William Toynbee, Pierre Jean de Béranger

Songs of Béranger

William Toynbee, Pierre Jean de Béranger

Songs of Béranger

ISBN/EAN: 9783337020323

Printed in Europe, USA, Canada, Australia, Japan

Cover: Foto ©Andreas Hilbeck / pixelio.de

More available books at **www.hansebooks.com**

SONGS OF BÉRANGER. TRANSLATED INTO ENGLISH VERSE BY WILLIAM TOYNBEE.

LONDON:

WALTER SCOTT, LIMITED,

24 WARWICK LANE.

NEW YORK: 3 EAST FOURTEENTH STREET.

CONTENTS.

— •••

PREFACE.

———•◦•———

PIERRE JEAN DE BÉRANGER was born on the
19th August 1780, and died on the 16th July
1857. His life extended over the most mo-
mentous period of his country's history; he
witnessed the storming of the Bastille, and he
refused a pension from the Second Empire.

If in the highest sense of the word something
less than a Poet, Béranger was indisputably the
prince of Singers. Teeming with the keenest
of satire, the tenderest of pathos, the archest of
gaiety, it was from Humankind that he invari-
ably drew his inspiration. Tears and Laughter,
Love and Friendship, Glory and Heroism, above

all, Liberty, were the themes on which he rang
the changes with inexhaustible fire and sweet-
ness. Sprung from the People,—a fact in which
he never ceased to exult—it was of and to the
People that he loved best to sing. His every
note found an echo in their hearts. He soothed
their sorrows, he sympathised with their joys, he
kindled their patriotism. To France he was
infinitely more than even Burns was to Scotland,
or Moore to Ireland; the spell of his song was
unparalleled, and, perhaps, Posterity could
award him no fitter title than that of the last
and greatest of National Minstrels.

To those who are able to read Béranger in
his own exquisite language these translations
are not addressed, but any who lack that ad-
vantage may, it is hoped, derive from them some
impression, however faint, if not of the Singer,
at least of the Man. Several of these renderings
appeared in a smaller selection published a few

years ago, but for reasons which will be readily understood, the songs paraphrased by Mr. Thackeray were left untouched. These have now been attempted, not from any diminished diffidence on the part of the translator, but because in a series which, like the present, aims at being representative, the songs in question could not properly be omitted.

W. T.

SONGS OF BÉRANGER.

———•••———

MY COAT.

My humble friend, forsake me not '
   We both are ageing by degrees ;
I've brushed you ten long years, a lot
   Worthy of even Socrates !
When upon evil days you fall,
   And holes in dire profusion start,
Like me, be sternly Stoical !
   My dear old coat, we'll never part !

Well can I recollect the day
   When Destiny first made you mine,
Comrades were gathered round me gay,
   To keep my fête with song and wine ;

Your poverty—'twas, too, my pride—
  Has caused me not a single smart;
Those friends still rally to my side;
  My dear old coat, we'll never part!

You boast a darn, which to the last
  I lovingly shall call to mind;
One night, from Rose retreating fast,
  I felt a sudden snatch behind!
We tussled, you were torn in two;
  It cost her dear that desperate dart,
She took a week to tinker you!
  My dear old coat, we'll never part!

By perfumes you were ne'er defiled
  Such as infest a coxcomb's glass,
Into no ante-room beguiled
  Where courtiers sycophantic pass;
When France to Stars resigned her soul,
  For Ribands made an open mart,
A daisy decked your button-hole!—
  My dear old coat, we'll never part!

Ah, well, we've little more to fear,
    Our chequered course will soon be run,
There'll soon be truce to smile and tear,
    To shadow interspersed with sun !
For the last garb of all, good friend,
    I must prepare to nerve my heart ;
No matter ! we'll together end,
    My dear old coat, we'll never part !

THE BROKEN FIDDLE.

EAT away, my poor dog, eat away,
  Never mind if I can't take my share;
There's just a cake left for to-day,
  And to-morrow on crusts we must fare !

The foreigner cut-throats last night,
  As I played on the green to our folk,
Cried, "A dance !"   I refused, so in spite
  My poor fiddle to pieces they broke.

'Twas the band of the village !   Farewell,
  Joyous fêtes, happy days ! ne'er again
Will it quicken the foot of the belle,
  Or embolden the heart of the swain !

How merrily on marriage morn,
  As the bridegroom stood waiting to hear,
From its string would the signal be borne
  That the bride was at last drawing near !

Not the sternest of priests could resent
  The frolics it roused in the ring,
And one strain of its sweet merriment
  Would have smoothed e'en the brow of a king!

If it tuned in our glory's full glow
  Now and then to a soul-stirring song,
Little dreamed I the foreigner's blow
  Would requite it one day for the wrong!

Eat away, my poor dog, eat away,
  Never mind if I can't take my share;
There's just a cake left for to-day,
  And to-morrow on crusts we must fare!

Ah, how saddened in barn and in field
  On a Sunday will now be the scene!
And how think you the vintage will yield,
  When I fiddle no more as they glean?

At its music the poor ceased to brood;
  The most dreary of toil 'twould relax,
And bring solace, when nothing else could,
  For oppressor, and tempest, and tax!

It subdued the fierce workings of hate,
  Stayed the tear, howe'er bitter its flow;
Ah! believe me, no sceptre of state
  E'er did half so much good as my bow!

Well, the cut-throat I'll thank to his face,
  For the courage at last he's awoke;
A stout blade shall to-morrow replace
  The poor fiddle he yesterday broke!

And they'll say, if I perish perchance,
  "Ah, his tunes were the life of our sward,
Till the foreigner called for a dance,
  Then he flung down his bow for the sword!"

Eat away, my poor dog, eat away,
  Never mind if I can't take my share;
There's just a cake left for to-day,
  And to-morrow on crusts we must fare!

TO MY FRIENDS BECOME MINISTERS.

No, no, my friends, my wants are few,
   Elsewhere with your good things make free;
Courts may be well enough for you,
   But spread no royal snare for me.
All that I ask is Love's caress,
   Blithe comrades, and a crust of bread;
Bending my lowly cot to bless,
   " Be nothing," the Almighty said.

Splendour would but embarrass me,
   Who idly sing from day to day;
Were Fortune's crumbs my share to be,
   " I've never earned them," I should say;
On honest Labour's humble board
   More fitly far they would be spread ;
At least my wallet's amply stored !
   "Be nothing," the Almighty said.

One day upwafted in a dream,
  From Heav'n I gazed down on the world;
There, all in one vast living stream
  Were monarchs, nations, armies swirled;
I heard a shout, 'twas Victory's strain;
  One name from realm to realm was sped—
Ye Great, and thus your glories wane!
  "Be nothing," the Almighty said.

Nevertheless, all praise to you,
  Intrepid pilots of the realm,
Who bidding each his ease adieu,
  Haste to the storm-struck vessel's helm;
"Good luck," I holloa from the shore,
  "Right nobly may you speed ahead!"
Then in the sun I bask once more—
  "Be nothing," the Almighty said.

Your graves will be superb, no doubt,
  Mine but a nameless mound of grass;
Crape-covered crowds will see you out,
  I in a pauper's hearse shall pass;

Yet, to us all doom is but doom,
   Your glow is quenched, my glimmer fled,
The only difference is the tomb !
   " Be nothing," the Almighty said.

Then, let me be myself once more,
   To pomp I make my last salute,
Behind your grandly-gilded door
   I've left my hobnails and my flute !
Tho' Freedom, to us both so sweet,
   Your painted halls need never dread,
I'll pipe her praises in the street !—
   " Be nothing," the Almighty said.

HORRID SPRING.

WE'VE loved the whole long winter now,
    She at that window, I at this;
But if we love, we never bow,
    And only at a distance kiss !
Thro' the bare branches of that plane,
    It was our one delight to peer,
And now it's almost green again !—
    Spring, are you coming every year?

Yes, she's been spirited away,
    The charming angel I espied
Relieving, the first frosty day,
    Her feathered pensioners outside.
'Twas time to love, I used to know,
    The instant I saw them appear;
If I adore one thing, it's snow !—
    Spring, are you coming every year?

But for you, I might watch her still,
  Each morning as she hastes to rise,
As fresh as ever painter's skill
  Reveals Aurora to our eyes ;
But for you, I might still exclaim,
  " The setting of my star is near ;
She sleeps ; I miss her candle's flame."—
  Spring, are you coming every year?

Oh, for the winter back again !
  If only I could hear once more
The sharp hail crackle on the pane,
  And see it fretted with the hoar !
A fig for all your fabled wiles !
  Buds and long days may cost too dear ;
Haven't they robbed me of her smiles ?—
  Spring, are you coming every year?

THE GARRET.

YES, here's the old room where I roughed it so long
  In the penniless days I ne'er cease to regret,
When a scapegrace of twenty I lived but for song,
  A few cheery friends, and the charms of Lisette!
In the prime of Life's spring-tide, ne'er taking
    account
  Of the world and its ways, or what Fate had in
    store,
How gaily up six flights of stairs would I mount !
  Ah, give me my youth and a garret once more !

A garret ! the fact I am proud to confess !
  Over there stood the pallet which served as a bed,
Here tottered my table, and can it be? yes,
  On the wall a rude stanza is still to be read !
Dear simple delights of Life's rose-tinted dawn,
  Too soon by Time's tyranny doomed to be o'er,
How often my watch for your sake would I pawn !—
  Ah, give me my youth and a garret once more !

See, here comes Lisette tripping airily in,
    A flower in her bonnet coquettishly twined,
How pretty she looks standing tiptoe to pin
    Her shawl o'er the window in place of a blind !
Thanks, too, to the skirt she slips laughingly down,
    The lack of a quilt we've no need to deplore ;
(I didn't know then who had paid for the gown !)
    Ah, give me my youth and a garret once more !

Then that carnival night, when beginning to troll
    Some boisterous carol of folly and fun,
We heard the far boom of artillery roll—
    Napoleon had vanquished ; Marengo was won !
How it broke into triumph our bacchanal song,
    Mighty France our one theme, and the Laurels
        she wore !
Where were now all the kings who had braved her
        so long ?
    Ah, give me my youth and a garret once more !

Farewell, beloved scenes of a long-vanished past,
    Whose every bright moment 'tis bliss to recall !
Were my years ev'n a century longer to last,
    For one hour of those days I would barter them all!

Magic era of Glory and Love and Delight,
  When the whole of Life's wine at one banquet
    we pour,
And the Iris of Hope seems forever in sight !—
  Ah, give me my youth and a garret once more !

THE VAGABOND.

THIS ditch will do ; yes, here I'll die!
  Could Misery find a fitter grave?
They'll think I'm drunk, the passers-by ;
  Let them, and so their pity save !
Some with a sneer will turn away,
  Some toss me possibly a "sou" !—
On to the fair I don't mind me, pray;
  Why should my dying trouble you?

Yes, I am dying of old age,
  For hunger never kills, you see !
I'd hoped the workhouse might assuage
  My last few hours of misery ;
But every workhouse overflows,
  Such numbers are like me forlorn :
So in the gutter, I suppose,
  I'll have to die, as I was born !

When young, the workmen I would pray
   To teach me how to earn my bread;
"What! when for ours we scarce can pay?
   Off to the streets and beg!" they said.
"Work," said the rich; but, there, I own,
   Upon their straw I've often lain,
Grubbed from their dung-heaps many a bone,
   So of the rich I can't complain!

I could have been a thief, I knew,
   But I preferred to beg, somehow;
At times I've snatched an apple, true,
   From off an overhanging bough;
But in his Majesty's snug cell
   I've pretty dearly had to pay!
I had at least the sun; ah! well,
   They even took the sun away!

What country have the poor to claim?
   What profit us your wine and corn,
Your commerce, your immortal fame,
   Your hosts of statesmen heaven-born?

When on your smoking walls last year
  The foreigner loot-laden stood,
Think you for France I shed that tear?
  No, 'twas because he gave me food !

Better to crush us 'neath your heel,
  As you crush Nature's crawling scum,
Than only let us live to feel
  What by your aid we might become !
Once sheltered from the nipping blast,
  The grub grows to the ant, and I
My blessings on you might have cast—
  Now, hear me curse you as I die !

THE OLD COLOURS.

SURROUNDED by the comrades brave
  Of many and many a glorious fight,
  Over the kindling wine to-night
I summoned memory from the grave.
And while each field anew we fought,
  Yon drooping colours met my eye;
" Ah, shall I ne'er again," methought,
  " See them unfurled before I die?"

Beneath my humble thatch they hang,
  A worn-out veteran's single prize ;
  Emblem of countless victories,
Whose fame thro' all creation rang !
For twenty years with glory fraught
  From field to field they waved on high ;
" Ah, shall I ne'er again," methought,
  " See them unfurled before I die?"

To France they fifty-fold repaid
  The blood that set her brave sons free ;
  Upon the lap of Liberty
Our babes their lance a plaything made !

Gaze on them, tyrants, and be taught
 How glory like a gleam flits by !
"Ah, shall I ne'er again," methought,
 "See them unfurled before I die?"

Their Eagle in the dust lies low,
 Wearied with battle's ceaseless shock ;
 But have we not the Gallic Cock
Who braved of old so many a foe?
No longer by defeat distraught
 Once more we'll hoist them by-and-by ;
"Ah, shall I ne'er again," methought,
 "See them unfurled before I die?"

If shorn awhile of Victory's pride,
 So long their appanage, what then?
 Each soldier is a citizen ;
They'll still be found on Duty's side !
France, to the verge of ruin brought,
 With new-born hope they shall supply ;
"Ah, shall I ne'er again," methought,
 "See them unfurled before I die?"

And here, in my poor hovel here,
 They hang upon this very wall !—
 My flag, my pride, my hope, my all.
Come wipe away a soldier's tear !
A soldier's tear !   O thus besought,
 Can Heav'n my humble prayer deny?
No, no, once more—ah ! glorious thought,
 I'll see you float before I die !

OFF TO THE COUNTRY.

Up from your pillow, graceless Rose,
  Daybreak at last begins to peer,
At last yon solemn chimes disclose
  The hour you promised to be here.
Far from the city's whirl and heat
We'll with our happiness retreat ;
Yes, to the country let us rove,
And learn what it can teach of love !

The verdure of the Spring we'll press,
  Ranging the meadows hand in hand,
And taste that deeper tenderness
  Which Nature only can command.
The birds from every glen and glade
Call us to join them in the shade ;
Then to the country let us rove,
And learn what it can teach of love !

We'll live the village life, we two ;
  Daybreak shall see us gaily rise,
And with the first fall of the dew
  Slumber once more shall seal our eyes.

3

You'll hardly then complain, my Rose,
Of the long day that never goes!
Come, to the country let us rove,
And learn what it can teach of love!

When Summer to the golden fields
   Beckons the reaper once again,
And each stroke of the sickle yields
   The gleaner, too, her share of grain,
What stolen kisses won't we spy
Behind the tall sheaves, you and I?
Come, to the country let us rove,
And learn what it can teach of love!

As Autumn presses from the vine
   Its streams of nectar, by the vat
We'll sit and watch the bubbling wine,
   And listen to the old folks' chat,
Of old days dead, old ditties sung
When love was love, and they were young.
Come, to the country let us rove,
And learn what it can teach of love!

Along the river-banks we'll stray
   Just as one does in dreams, you know;
And ever as we roam away,
   More languid will your footsteps grow.
Beneath us cool the mosses are,
The grass is soft, the world afar !
Come, to the country let us rove,
And learn what it can teach of love !

We're off ! Parade and pomp, farewell !
   Paris, I turn my back on you ;
In art and splendour lies your spell,
   I worship one that you eschew.
Come, Rose, we'll veil from envious eyes
How to make earth a paradise !
Quick, to the country let us rove,
And learn what it can teach of love !

MY LITTLE CORNER.

No, life for me has lost its spell,
  All that I ask for now is rest;
Too long have I been doomed to dwell
  Where Pleasure only palls at best.
I've burst my bonds and got away,
  A galley-slave at last set free;
So leave me in my corner, pray,
  My little corner none can see!

There, daring Power to do its worst,
  I weigh the wrongs existence brings,
Weep for the nations tyrant-curst,
  Judge and pass sentence on the kings;
Boldly predicting Freedom's sway,
  The future's page I scan with glee;
Then leave me in my corner, pray,
  My little corner none can see!

There, with a wizard's wand endowed,
  For good alone I use my trust,
Erect to Justice trophies proud,
  And every palace doom to dust;

I've monarchs, but no despots they,
   "Love and be loved" is their decree;
Then leave me in my corner, pray,
   My little corner none can see!

There on light wings my spirit soars
   And, fluttering a cherub blithe,
Laughs to behold earth's emperors
   In everlasting torment writhe!
One only basks in Glory's ray,
   My song's immortal hero, he;
Then leave me in my corner, pray,
   My little corner none can see!

Thus for my country do I scheme
   Plans to which Heav'n gives willing heed;
Then let me unmolested dream,
   Your giddy world no more I need;
The muse, should Fortune go astray,
   The muse will take good care of me;
So leave me in my corner, pray,
   My little corner none can see!

THE BOXERS; or, ANGLO-MANIA.
(1814.)

WHEN not required his hat to scan,
"God-dam!" I like your Englishman;
   He's so refined in character,
Is so polite, has always graced
His pleasures with such perfect taste!
Well, let's hope we. as we advance,
May worship fisticuffs in France
   As they do in proud old England, Sir!

Picture the boxers over here!
First we've our bets to book, that's clear,
   A notary by, in case we err!
A real fight this, if you want fun,
And not their favourite two to one!
Well, let's hope we, as we advance,
May worship fisticuffs in France
   As they do in proud old England, Sir!

That's it! and now just please admire
These gentlemen, their choice attire,
   Their grace, what could be gracefuller?

"A brace of butchers!" some one sneers?
I'll wager they're a brace of peers!
Well, let's hope we, as we advance,
May worship fisticuffs in France
   As they do in proud old England, Sir!

There, ladies, what d'you say to that?
For you as arbiters have sat;
   What, to applaud them you demur?
Look at that blood, and then refrain!
God! aren't your Englishmen humane!
Well, let's hope we, as we advance,
May worship fisticuffs in France
   As they do in proud old England, Sir!

England, we'll copy you post-haste,
Your laws, your fashions, your good taste,
   Ev'n to your strategy defer!
When we've done envying, that is,
Your horseflesh and your embassies!
Well, let's hope we, as we advance,
May worship fisticuffs in France
   As they do in proud old England, Sir!

THE VILLAGE EPICUREAN.

TAKE note of this, ye gentry who
    Your self-made sorrows mourn !
Unblest with ev'n a single "sou"
    Blithe Pierre le Gros was born ;
At ease to live, eschewing fame,
    Of discontent the foe—
Such, Sirs, the modest end and aim
    Of jolly Pierre le Gros !

A hat, the product you'd suppose
    Of his great-grandsire's day,
With ivy now, and now with rose
    Perennially gay !
A suit of sacking, first possest
    Some twenty years ago—
Such, Sirs, the wardrobe at its best
    Of jolly Pierre le Gros !

A pack of cards, a flageolet,
    A table, an old bed,
An empty chest, a silhouette
    (His sweetheart's be it said) ;

A jug which Providence takes care
   Shall never cease to flow—
Such, Sirs, the utmost wealth can spare
   To jolly Pierre le Gros !

Instructor to the little folk
   In games of every kind,
Profuse with pleasantry and joke
   More racy than refined ;
In country dance and catch and glee
   His knowledge prompt to show—
Such, Sirs, the whole proficiency
   Of jolly Pierre le Gros !

Since costly brands he cannot get,
   Content with common wine,
Preferring chubby-cheeked Nannette
   To damsels superfine ;
With loving-kindness brimming o'er,
   With harmless mirth aglow—
Such, Sirs, the philosophic lore
   Of jolly Pierre le Gros !

Humbly to fall upon his knees
  And to his Father say,
" Pardon me if my life displease
  By being a thought too gay ;
I ask but till the end to share
  The bliss that now I know "—
Such, Sirs, the unpretending prayer
  Of jolly Pierre le Gros !

Ye Poor, who filled with envy fret,
  Ye Rich, whose pleasures pall,
Ye Great, who striving more to get
  Too oft are stript of all ;
Ye kings, who see your crowns depart,
  Your dynasties laid low,
A lesson learn and learn by heart
  From jolly Pierre le Gros !

POLAND !

How would I live my life again?
  Why, Mars this time should be my star ;
I'd get a fierce moustache in train,
    And be a dare-devil Hussar !
    Not such as yon sword-danglers are !
No, like the wind you'd see me spur
    And charge for Poland's hapless brave !
What, and France too must play the cur?
    Up, and wake Honour from the grave !

Ah, had this heart its once high beat,
    I'd win the fairest of the fair,
Just to say " To your saddle, sweet,
    As is the way with women there !
    What they have dared, you too shall dare !
Sell trinkets, gewgaws, all, no stint ;
    And, while there's still a life to save,
Strip all your linen into lint ! "
    Up, and wake Honour from the grave !

More—could I lay hands on the gold,
　　I'd scour Sarmatia with the cry,
" Rally your legions, lion-souled,
　　Arms, ammunition, all, I'll buy,
　　Name but your needs, and I'll supply!
For Europe, who her carcase drags
　　On crutches, Wealth's decrepit slave,
Revolts at Valour in her rags!"
　　Up, and wake Honour from the grave!

Were I a king, the Muscovite
　　Would hardly find my squadrons loth!
Their every blade should bare for fight,
　　And shame the Crescent from its sloth!
　　Sweden should rise, and flanked by both,
" Poland!" I'd cry, "our flag's unfurled,
　　And this, the sceptre that I wave,
Can reach the confines of the world!"
　　Up, and wake Honour from the grave!

Ah, could I be for one brief hour
　　That God whom Poland kneels before,
How think you first I'd prove my power?
　　The Czar should see the dawn no more!
　　Yes, I'd be Poland's to the core!

With miracles (for such she needs),
  With miracles her path I'd pave,
And quench the stars her conqueror reads !
  Up, and wake Honour from the grave !

Up ! but of what avail to dream ?—
  Great King of Liberty, befriend !
O'er Poland in her hour supreme
  From Thy far throne of Justice bend !
  Make me her guardian-angel ! Lend
To my faint song Thy Voice profound,
  Till earth and all the seas that lave
Earth's every shore, one anthem sound,
  " Up, and wake Honour from the grave ! "

EPIGRAM.

(Written on a collection of MS. verses.)

IF I were a king, king of catch and of song,
  As is whispered sometimes in my ear,
Your redoubtable muse would before very long
  Prove a dangerous rival, I fear.
For the precepts she lays so impressively down
  To the People, that pestilent thing,
Would one of these days play the deuce with my
    crown,
      If I were a king !

MY CURÉ.

OUR Curé's busied o'er the task
Of emptying last season's cask
　　Now that the Autumn's near ;
And blessing God, with man at peace,
Thus he harangues his little niece
　　(Just turned her sixteenth year):
" Bring me no tales ; what use to fret ?
Those whom the Devil wants he'll get !
　　So there, there, there, God's will be done !
　　Give me a kiss, my pretty one,
　　And let us be hard on none !

" 'Tis only for the wolves I keep
A rod in pickle, for poor sheep
　　Who would a scourge employ ?
No, no, say I, take my advice,
Peace is a very Paradise
　　Each of us may enjoy !
Then above all my code ordains
Never to preach except it rains !

So there, there, there, God's will be done !
Give me a kiss, my pretty one,
And let us be hard on none !

" On Sundays should my flock be bent
On seeking pleasures innocent
    I seldom interfere.
And if in church (where oft, *entre nous,*
I'm priest and congregation too !)
    Their revelry I hear,
Why, I step over to the inn
And beg for just a shade less din.
    So there, there, there, God's will be done !
    Give me a kiss, my pretty one,
    And let us be hard on none !

" If, as my daily rounds I ply,
A case of frailty I espy,
    The fact I don't proclaim.
Who's free from sin, when all is said ?
And if a moon too late they wed,
    I've not the heart to blame ;

Moralists, doubtless, fault will find,
But Heav'n and Suzanne will not mind!
  So there, there, there, God's will be done!
  Give me a kiss, my pretty one,
  And let us be hard on none!

"Our mayor, a trifle lax in creed,
Lends to my sermons little heed,
  But ah, he'll be forgiven!
For 'tis a fact, as well I know,
That with both hands he loves to sow,
  Observed of none save Heaven!
God of his deeds will record keep,
As he has sown he too shall reap!
  So there, there, there, God's will be done!
  Give me a kiss, my pretty one,
  And let us be hard on none!

"At every dinner I preside,
Flowers for my fête-day all provide,
  My cask ne'er wants for wine;
Embittered with a bigot's gloom
Our Bishop prophesies my doom,—
  But ah, may it be mine

Some day in yonder Land of Rest
To meet all those I here have blest !
  So there, there, there, God's will be done !
  Give me a kiss, my pretty one,
  And let us be hard on none ! "

THE SWALLOWS.

A PRISONER on Morocco's shore
  Thus from his chains was heard to sigh :
"Ah, do I gaze on you once more,
  Ye birds that from the winter fly?
Bright swallows whom, as on ye glance,
  Hope heralds o'er the burning sand ;
Surely you must have flown from France,
  And tell me of my native land !

"How oft I've prayed you just to bring
  One blossom from the far-off vale,
Where in my boyhood's joyous Spring,
  The future told so fair a tale !
Beside a flowering lilac tree,
  Where a brook's ripples idly roam,
Our cottage you must often see !
  Ah, now you tell me of my home !

"Some nest of yours may chance to lie
  Close to the room where I was born,
And there you've heard the plaintive cry
  Wrung from a mother's heart forlorn,

On yonder door her gaze she keeps,
  Waiting in vain to see it move,
And when I come not, how she weeps !
  Ah, now you tell me of her love !

" My sister, is she married yet ?
  And did you watch our village-folk
From daybreak till the sun had set
  Keeping her fête beneath the oak ?
My playmates, too, who with me learned
  How soon Youth's dream of glory ends ;
Have any to their homes returned ?
  Ah, now you tell me of my friends !

" No, o'er their corpses marching back,
  The conqueror thro' our vale careers,
Beside my hearth to bivouac,
  And fill my sister's home with tears !
My mother's voice no more I hear,
  My days beneath these fetters close ;
Ah, swallows of my country dear,
  You tell me only of my woes ! "

GOOD-NIGHT!

WITH a clink, dear old friend, with a clink,
    To the rapturous days that are dead,
To the days of our youth let us drink,
    And sigh for each pleasure that's sped !
Yet not in despondency, no !
    With laughter we'll put her to flight !
When it's time for us, comrade, to go,
    Let it be with a merry good-night !

Fifty winters you've weathered it here,
    Mine also are fast flitting on,
Yet have they not wholly been drear,
    For each shadow a sunbeam has shone !
Had riches rained on us their flow,
    Would they, think you, have bettered our
        plight?
When it's time for us, comrade, to go,
    Let it be with a merry good-night !

With the muses you put me to nurse,
    I've eclipsed you, yet little you care ;
Tho' denied every blessing but verse,
    Could we change it for any more fair?

In our carols the Past with its glow
   Shall waken again into sight ;
When it's time for us, comrade, to go,
   Let it be with a merry good-night !

But see, it grows dark, and no doubt,
   Gay Cupid our playmate of yore,
Should he happen to spy us will shout,
   " Your day, my fine fellows, is o'er ! "
But Friendship will not flout us so,
   Thro' the gloom she will guide with her light ;
When it's time for us, comrade, to go,
   Let it be with a merry good-night !

AN EPICUREAN'S PRAYER.

LOVE, tho' from thy full harvest-field
    Death plucks the golden grain,
Oh, thaw the hearts by grief congealed,
    And kindle them again.
Against the promptings of despair
    Let thy sweet impulse plead,
And if the harvest Death must share,
    Cease not to sow the seed !

THE GRANDMOTHER'S TALE.

His fame shall never pass away !
  Beside the cottage-hearth the hind
  No other theme shall list to find
For many and many a distant day.
When winter nights their gloom begin,
  And winter embers ruddy glow,
Round some old gossip closing in,
  They'll beg a tale of long ago—
" For all," they'll say, "he wrought us ill,
  His glorious name shall ne'er grow dim,
The people love, yes, love him still,
  So, Grandmother, a tale of him,
            A tale of him !"

" One day past here I saw him ride,
  A caravan of kings behind ;
  The time I well can call to mind,
I hadn't then been long a bride.
I gazed out from the open door,
  Slowly his charger came this way ;
A little hat, I think, he wore,
  Yes, and his riding coat was grey.

I shook all over as quite near,
   Close to this very door he drew-
'Good-day,' he cried, 'good-day, my
      dear!' "—
  "What, Grandmother, he spoke to you,
      He spoke to you?"

"The following year I chanced to be
   In Paris; every street was gay,
   He'd gone to Notre Dame to pray,
And passed again quite close to me!
The sun shone out in all its pride,
   With triumph every bosom swelled,
'Ah, what a glorious scene!' they cried,
   'Never has France the like beheld!'
A smile his features seemed to wear,
   As on the crowds his glance he threw,
For he'd an heir, at last, an heir!"—
  "Ah, Grandmother, what times for you,
      What times for you!"

"Then came for France that dreadful day
   When foes swept over all the land;
   Undaunted he alone made stand,
As tho' to keep the world at bay!—

One winter's night, as this might be,
  I heard a knocking at the door;
I opened it ; great heavens ! 'twas he !
  A couple in his wake, no more ;
Then sinking down upon a seat,
  Ay, 'twas upon this very chair,
He gasped 'Defeat ! ah God, defeat !'"—
  "What, Grandmother, he sat down *there*,
          He sat down *there?*"

"He called for food ; I quickly brought
  The best I happened to have by;
Then when his dripping clothes were dry,
He seemed to doze awhile, methought;
Seeing me weeping when he woke,
  'Courage,' he cried, 'there's still a chance;
I go to Paris, one bold stroke,
  And Paris shall deliver France !'
He went ; the glass I'd seen him hold,
  The glass to which his lips he'd set,
I've treasured since like gold, like gold !"—
  "How, Grandmother, you have it yet,
          You have it yet?"

" 'Tis there.   But all, alas, was o'er ;
  He, whom the Pope himself had crown'd,
  The mighty hero world-renown'd,
Died prisoner on a far-off shore.
For long we none believed the tale,
  They said that he would reappear,
Across the seas again would sail,
  To fill the universe with fear !
But when we found that he was dead,
  When all the shameful truth we knew,
The bitter, bitter tears I shed ! "—
  " Ah, Grandmother, God comfort you,
          God comfort you ! "

ROSETTE.

WHAT! all oblivious of your youth,
   On me your myriad spells you'd ply,
Who, to confess the fatal truth,
   Have seen full forty summers fly!
On me, whose one flame hitherto
   Has been a cotton-gowned coquette!
Ah, if I only could love you
   As once I used to love Rosette!

Your carriage whirls you every day
   In satins—who can guess their worth?
Rosette with just a riband gay
   Skimmed laughingly her mother-earth,
While right and left her glances flew
   To keep me in a constant pet!
Ah, if I only could love you
   As once I used to love Rosette!

As down your velvet pile you pass,
   Grand mirrors greet you everywhere;
Rosette had but one looking-glass,
   The Graces must have put it there!

No damask round her bed she drew,
  Her sleep the sun could never fret !
Ah, if I only could love you
  As once I used to love Rosette !

You've earned, thanks to your pretty wit,
  More than one poetaster's meed ;
Well, I'll unblushingly admit,
  Rosette knew scarcely how to read,
But Cupid always pulled her through,
  If in a fix she chanced to get.
Ah, if I only could love you
  As once I used to love Rosette !

In looks she came behind you far,
  Nor indeed had she half your heart ;
Those eyes of yours much gentler are
  When a poor lover lisps his part !
But Youth, bright Youth, a glamour threw
  Over her charms which glimmers yet—
Ah no, I never can love you
  As once I used to love Rosette !

MY TOMB.

What, for me in the pink of good health,
  A magnificent tomb you project?
Not to Poverty, friends, but to Wealth,
  Should be proffered such marks of respect!
If your homage you hanker to pay,
  This shape let the tribute assume—
In the finest Lafitte or Tokay,
  Let us drink out the price of my tomb!

For the cost of my sculptured renown
  (I conclude you would do the thing well!),
A twelvemonth or more out of town
  In Arcadian peace I might dwell;
Or, since my poor larder's supply
  For improvement leaves plenty of room,
In good dinners, the best you can buy,
  Let us eat up the price of my tomb!

I'm old, older far than Babette,
  An ordeal she endeavours to bear;
On the races her heart she has set,
  But she hasn't a frock fit to wear;

If her wardrobe you'd kindly renew,
  To resent it I shouldn't presume;
In rewarding devotion so true,
  Let us lavish the price of my tomb!

At Eternity's drama, my friends,
  In no box I'm ambitious to pose;
Yonder beggar who death-stricken bends,
  Let us gladden his heart ere he goes!
In the shining Arena he'll sit,
  Long before I've emerged from the gloom:
To retain me a place in the pit,
  Let us pay him the price of my tomb!

I ask for no epitaph fine,
  To mystify pedants unborn,
Nor one flower of to-day would resign
  For the wreaths that a coffin adorn;
Posterity (if it's to be!)
  No lamp for my sake need illume,
For to the last stiver, you see,
  I've expended the price of my tomb!

THE BEGGAR-WOMAN.

WHERE the snowflakes whirl over yonder flags
   A woman kneels hand-outspread,
The ice-wind pierces her wretched rags
   As she prays,—can it be for bread?
Those cathedral gates are her daily goal,
   Let the weather be what it may,
And, saddest of all, she is blind, poor soul;
   For pity's sake turn not away!

Know you what she was once, that woman there,
   So haggard and broken-down?
At the opera none was a tithe so fair,
   And her voice was the talk of the town;
Let her move them to laughter or melt to tears,
   Their homage all flocked to pay;
Day and night she bewitched them, heart, eyes,
      and ears.
   For pity's sake turn not away!

How often, as swiftly her carriage swept
   From the stage-door, would she hear
The crowd that had worshipped, as out she stept,
   Speed her homeward with cheer on cheer!

And then when she deigned to go out and sup,
  What a bevy of gallants gay
Would compete for the honour of handing her up!
  For pity's sake turn not away!

What a triumph was hers when its emblems rare
  Were proffered by every art!
What bronzes, what marbles, what gems were
    there,
  Fond tributes from heart to heart!
At her banquets how Flattery's fair-weather
    throng,
  As the wine in each breast made play,
Would ply her with plaudit and toast and song!
  For pity's sake turn not away!

Ah, the terrible change! in one hour she lost,
  At one blow, both voice and sight,
And lonely and poor on the world was tossed
  To beg as she begs to-night.
Twenty years have I watched that imploring hand,
  Whose alms in Prosperity's day
No suppliant ever were known to withstand.
  For pity's sake turn not away!

More wildly than ever down whirls the snow,
  Her limbs are benumbed with cold,
And the beads she has now grown to fondle so
  Her fingers can scarcely hold.
May her gentle heart 'neath its weight of woes
  Still summon up strength to pray,
Till she passes at last into Heaven's repose!
  For pity's sake turn not away!

THE LITTLE MAN IN GREY.

IN Paris there's a little man all dressed in dapple
  grey,
With chubby cheeks and cheery heart he goes upon
  his way,
And when he peers into his purse and finds there's
  nothing there,
Instead of being in doleful dumps he simply doesn't
  care !

> " For you see," chirrups he,
>   This merry mannikin,
> " The only way to be gay
>   Is not to care a pin !
> Not to care, not to care,
>   Not to care a pin ! "

What with a relish for good wine, and weakness
  for grisettes,
He's managed somehow to incur a tidy crop of
  debts,

But when the bailiff and the dun he meets upon
the stair,
Instead of quaking in his shoes he simply doesn't
care !

"For you see," chirrups he,
This merry mannikin,
"The only way to be gay
Is not to care a pin !
Not to care, not to care,
Not to care a pin !"

When thro' the roof the rain at night drips down
upon his bed,
And on a well-drenched pillow-case he plumps his
hapless head,
When, pinched with cold, returning home, he finds
the scuttle bare,
Instead of cursing right and left, he simply doesn't
care !

"For you see," chirrups he,
This merry mannikin,
"The only way to be gay
Is not to care a pin !
Not to care, not to care,
Not to care a pin !"

When underneath his tattered quilt he's tortured
    with the gout,
And by his side the priest proceeds his errors to
    point out,
Exhorting him to mend his ways or for the worst
    prepare,
Instead of turning penitent he simply doesn't care !

      " For you see," chirrups he,
        This merry mannikin,
      " The only way to be gay
        Is not to care a pin !
      Not to care, not to care,
        Not to care a pin ! "

"WHEN I AM GONE."

YOU will grow old ; ah yes, my sweet,
  Grow old, and I shall be no more.
Time flies for me now far more fleet
  Than in the days that I deplore.
Live when I'm gone, if God so will,
  But to my teaching still be true ;
And by your fireside falter still
  The songs I used to sing to you !

When musing what was once their spell
  Those features worn, that hair of snow,
The young folk fain would have you tell
  Who was the friend you mourn for so,
Paint them my love, how it could thrill,
  Its follies, ev'n the doubts it threw,
And by your fireside falter still
  The songs I used to sing to you !

They'll ask, "Was he so winning then ?"
  "I loved him," calmly you'll reply.
"Had he no faults this best of men ?"
  "None" you'll avow with kindling eye,

"And plaintively as it could trill,
  His lute," you'll say, "was joyous too!"
Then by your fireside falter still
  The songs I used to sing to you!

You whom I taught to weep for France,
  Tell those who then her banners bear,
How "Glory" was my utterance,
  And "Hope," when hers was all despair;
While Fortune, in a night turned chill,
  Our laurels never ceased to strew;
Yes, by your fireside falter still
  The songs I used to sing to you!

My dearest, when my frail renown
  Soothes sometimes your declining hours,
When with a trembling hand you crown
  My portrait every Spring with flowers,
Look up where safe from age and ill
  We'll meet at last beyond the blue,
And till we meet, ah, falter still,
  The songs I used to sing to you!

THE KING OF YVETOT.

THERE flourished once a potentate,
  Whom History doesn't name;
He rose at ten, retired at eight,
  And snored unknown to Fame!
A night-cap for his crown he wore,
  A common cotton thing,
Which Jeannette to his bedside bore,
  This jolly little king!
Ho, ho, ho, ho! Ha, ha, ha, ha!
  This jolly little king!

With four diurnal banquets he
  His appetite allayed,
And on a jackass leisurely
  His royal progress made.
No cumbrous state his steps would clog,
  Fear to the winds he'd fling;
His single escort was a dog,
  This jolly little king!
Ho, ho, ho, ho! Ha, ha, ha, ha!
  This jolly little king!

He owned to only one excess,—
   He doted on his glass,—
But when a king gives happiness,
   Why that, you see, will pass!
On every bottle, small or great,
   For which he used to ring,
He laid a tax inordinate,
   This jolly little king!
Ho, ho, ho, ho! Ha, ha, ha, ha!
   This jolly little king!

Such crowds of pretty girls he found
   Occasion to admire,
It gave his subjects double ground
   For greeting him as Sire!
To shoot for cocoa-nuts he manned
   His army every Spring,
But all conscription sternly banned
   This jolly little king!
Ho, ho, ho, ho! Ha, ha, ha, ha!
   This jolly little king!

He eyed no neighbouring domain
   With envy or with greed,

And, like a pattern sovereign,
　Took Pleasure for his creed!
Yet, 'twas not, if aright I ween,
　Until his life took wing,
His subjects saw that he had been
　A jolly little king!
Ho, ho, ho, ho! Ha, ha, ha, ha!
　This jolly little king!

This worthy monarch, readers mine,
　You even now may see,
Embellishing a tavern-sign
　Well known to you and me!
There, when the fête-day bottle flows,
　Their bumpers they will bring,
And toast beneath his very nose
　This jolly little king!
Ho, ho, ho, ho! Ha, ha, ha, ha!
　This jolly little king!

THE MARQUIS OF CARABAS.
(1816.)

WHOM have we here in conqueror's *rôle ?*
Our grand old Marquis, bless his soul !
Whose grand old charger (mark his bone !)
Has borne him back to claim his own.
Note, if you please, the grand old style
In which he nears his grand old pile,
With what an air of grand old state
He waves that blade immaculate !

> Hats off, hats off, for my lord to pass,
> The grand old Marquis of Carabas !

" Ho ! almoners, chamberlains, appear !
Vassals, sub-vassals, serfs, I'm here,
I, the great Marquis, who alone
Replaced my monarch on his throne—
And now his Majesty's restored,
Let him my lawful rights accord !
If not, if he refuse to do it,
Corbleu ! his Majesty shall rue it ! "

> Hats off, hats off, for my lord to pass,
> The grand old Marquis of Carabas !

" Tho' on my blood to cast a slur,
They've hinted at a blacksmith, sir,
The head of my historic line
Sprang from the loins of Charlemagne !
Indeed, you'd in a twinkling see,
Could you but scan my pedigree,
That, matched with my descent, *parbleu*,
The King himself's a parvenu !"

Hats off, hats off, for my lord to pass,
The grand old Marquis of Carabas !

" Who to my claims shall dare demur ?
Marquise, you'll have the Bedchamber ;
Our second son shall take his pick,
Let's say, a good fat bishopric ;
Our first-born, the lord viscount, though
Not over-valiant, as we know,
Fancies a cross would meet his views ;
Well, he has only got to choose ! "

Hats off, hats off, for my lord to pass,
The grand old Marquis of Carabas !

"And now, for God's sake let me be !—
But who's that talks of taxing me?
Show me the code that dares create
A marquis debtor to the State !
Let them a single *sou* exact,
And by a round of grape-shot backed,
I'll teach them one of these fine days
To own the error of their ways !"

Hats off, hats off, for my lord to pass,
The grand old Marquis of Carabas !

"Priests, you have plenty to repair ;
Levy the tithes and let us share.
Brutes of the soil, I'll have you broke
To crouch once more beneath the yoke ;
And not a finger on the game !
Stay, there's one privilege you may claim :—
The first-fruits of your corn and wine
You're still allowed to add to mine !"

Hats off, hats off, for my lord to pass,
The grand old Marquis of Carabas !

" You, curé, to your office see !
Incense is my monopoly.
Varlets and pages, hearken well,
Belabour till the vermin yell !
For my posterity, be sure,
Shall every sacred right secure
Which (ere the Devil made the masses)
God granted to the Carabases ! "

Hats off, hats off, for my lord to pass,
The grand old Marquis of Carabas !

MARY STUART'S FAREWELL.

FAREWELL, farewell, thou beauteous clime,
  Scene of so many a joy gone by !
Land of my girlhood's golden prime,
  Farewell ! to leave thee is to die !

Homeless, in thee I found a home,
  From which I now afar must flee ;
But tho' to alien shores I roam,
  Ah, cease not to remember me !
The billows sweep the vessel's side,
  The wind is waking o'er the main,
Ah, why will Heaven not turn the tide,
  And give me back to thee again ?

Farewell, farewell, thou beauteous clime,
  Scene of so many a joy gone by !
Land of my girlhood's golden prime,
  Farewell ! to leave thee is to die !

When, lily-crown'd, thro' all the air
    I heard thy people's plaudits ring,
Was it because a queen stood there,
    Or Mary in her beauty's spring?
Of what avail to vaunt the sway
    Of Caledonia's drear domain?
Her sceptre I'd resign for aye
    To be one hour thy sovereign!

Farewell, farewell, thou beauteous clime,
    Scene of so many a joy gone by!
Land of my girlhood's golden prime,
    Farewell! to leave thee is to die!

'Mid Glory's glow, and Love's delight,
    My days have passed in bliss supreme,
But yon bleak wilderness of blight
    Will all too soon dispel the dream!
With coming ill my heart is fraught,
    Dread phantoms round my pillow flock;
Last night awaiting me, methought
    There loomed the scaffold and the block!

Farewell, farewell, thou beauteous clime,
   Scene of so many a joy gone by!
Land of my girlhood's golden prime,
   Farewell! to leave thee is to die!

Ah, France, my France, when doom draws near,
   When woe-begirt I end my days,
To thee who now my sobs dost hear,
   To thee I'll turn my weeping gaze!
Slowly the shore recedes from sight,
   Out o'er the surf my bark is tost,
And in the deepening gloom of night
   The last faint glimpse of thee is lost!

Farewell, farewell, thou beauteous clime,
   Scene of so many a joy gone by!
Land of my girlhood's golden prime,
   Farewell! to leave thee is to die!

THE MARIONETTES.

THE marionettes, my friends, I sing,
  Of every age the sport ;
Your peasant, no less than your king,
  In cottage and in court,
Lampooner, lacquey, sycophant,
  Prude, devotee, coquette,
(Not counting marionettes who rant !)
  Is each a marionette !

Man, flushed at finding he can walk,
  His power proceeds to boast ;
He here may strut, and there may stálk,
  So rules, forsooth, the roast !
Poor puppet, only let him wait
  Till Fortune's snares are set !
Come, my good sir, accept your fate,
  You're but a marionette !

That dainty pearl of innocence
  Love puts to such sweet pain,
Thrilling her heart-strings with a sense
  Her head cannot explain ;

All night awake, all day adream,
   Now tranced, now in a fret—
Ah, what a prize must Cupid deem
   That pretty marionette !

Yon gallant spouse Parisian
   Whom everybody greets,
Last night into your arms he ran,
   To-day he shuns the streets ;
Now jealousy he's fain to scout,
   Now fans a jealous pet—
He too, there's not the slightest doubt,
   Is but a marionette !

And what with Woman is our part ?
   Why, just a doll's well-wired !
"There, my fine fellow, off you start
   And jig until we're tired ! "
Ay, debonair or dunderhead,
   One treatment we all get—
Thank God, he's but a single thread,
   Your luckless marionette !

SPRING AND AUTUMN.

Two seasons in life reign supreme
  With all who to Pleasure incline;
In Spring we make flowers our one theme,
  In Autumn we vaunt but the vine.
Days lengthen—the rose has her spell ;
  They wane—for the vintage we sigh.
In Spring to the bottle farewell,
  In Autumn to Cupid good-bye!

'Twould be far more attractive, no doubt,
  The dual enjoyments to blend,
But the pace, as most people find out,
  Gets a trifle too brisk in the end ;
So in order sedately to dwell,
  I determined this system to try—
In Spring to the bottle farewell,
  In Autumn to Cupid good-bye !

In May I first chanced on Rosette,
  And succumbed in a trice to her smiles;
But she soon wore me out, the coquette,
  With her whims, and caprices, and wiles ;

Tho' I waited to fairly rebel
    Till October's first flagon ran dry—
In Spring to the bottle farewell,
    In Autumn to Cupid good-bye !

'Twas Belle who next wandered my way ;
    She provoked neither transport nor tear.
" I'm off," she informed me one day,
    And didn't come back for a year.
'Twas Autumn—said I : " Charming Belle,
    Here's a precept I always apply :—
In Spring to the bottle farewell,
    In Autumn to Cupid good-bye ! "

And now with a Houri I'm blest,
    Who my pleasures ordains at her will ;
To wine she imparts a new zest,
    To love she supplies a new thrill !
In short, the real truth if I tell,
    My rule she's resolved to defy—
To the bottle it's never farewell,
    To Cupid it's never good-bye !

ALL IN ALL.

WHATE'ER Philosophy may preach,
　I've a prodigious greed for gold !
Were Ophir's wealth within my reach,
　'Twould all at Adèle's feet be rolled !
To gratify her, in a trice
　O'er the four continents I'd flee !
I've not a spark of avarice,
　But Love—I dote on Love, you see !

A laureate's art I've been denied,
　But if, like some, I shone in rhyme,
Granting Adèle the theme supplied,
　My songs, I'm sure, would be sublime !
Our names in metre deftly knit
　Would be sufficient fame for me !
For glory I don't care a bit,
　But Love—I dote on Love, you see !

If ever Providence should place
　A crown on my plebeian head,
Why in that not too likely case,
　Adèle should wear it in my stead !

Even a levée-dress I'd sport,
  If so it pleased her to decree !
Ambition I disdain to court,
  But Love—I dote on Love, you see !

In sooth I've not a single need,
  Adèle to me is all in all ;
The best that Earth bestows, indeed,
  Compared with Love is bound to pall !
Heav'n for my happiness I thank ;
  From every freak of fortune free,
I've neither glory, wealth, nor rank ;
  But Love—I've boundless Love, you see !

EPIGRAM.

(Written in a lady's album.)

ON this album whenever you gaze,
  'Twill recall an old bard I'll not name,
Who, bewitched by your thousand sweet ways,
  Their dupe for a moment became.
Fell in love? not a whit! Love, the elf,
  Had long ago ceased to enthrall ;
He but took, vain old fool, to himself
  The sunshine you showered upon all !

PONIATOWSKI.

WHAT, flying ! you, the victors of the world !
    Hath Leipsic brought your vaunted hosts to bay ?
Flying ! and in the Elster's eddy swirled
    All the dire wreck and ruin of the fray !
Men, horses, arms, in headlong chaos thrown
    Athwart its flood, the river rages by,
Deaf to entreaty, sob, and shriek, and moan—
    "Help, Frenchmen, help, ah, leave me not to die !"

" Help ! who cries help? a curse on him !" they shout,
    " On, on, and if the hindmost falls, he falls !"
On, on they rush, ne'er pausing in the rout,
    Tho', pierced with wounds, 'tis Poniatowski calls!
Panic has stifled pity ; on they speed,
    No hand, no heart, responding to his cry ;
The ruthless torrent tears him from his steed—
    " Help, Frenchmen, help, ah, leave me not to die !"

He sinks—no, see, one desperate struggle more,
    And to the mane he clings with frenzied hold ;
"What, drown !" he cries, "while still upon the shore
    The bayonets clash, the cannon's boom is rolled !

Comrades ! your help ! my life has served your need,
How I have loved you let these wounds reply !
Save me, if but for France once more to bleed—
Help, Frenchmen, help, ah, leave me not to die ! "

On, on they sweep ; his hand lets loose the mane :
"Poland, my country, fare thee well !" he cries ;
And then there bursts upon his dying brain
A glorious vision wafted from the skies !
'Tis the White Eagle that at last awakes
And over slaughtered Russia swoops on high ;
Loud on his ear the hymn of victory breaks !—
"Help, Frenchmen, help, ah, leave me not to die ! "

In vain—one last faint gasp, and he is gone,—
The enemy bivouacs by the Elster's reeds—
Years have rolled past but still, as day grows wan,
A voice from those lone waters wildly pleads,
A voice which, floating up thro' Heaven's far gates,
By God is echoed back from out the sky,
Till with its anguish Earth reverberates,
"Help, Frenchmen, help, ah, leave me not to die ! "

'Tis Poland's supplication that we hear !
    Poland, that hath for France so often bled,
Poland, who for the honour she holds dear,
    Unmurmuringly her blood's last drop hath shed!
Like him who in the Elster's flood that day
    Perished for France without one helper nigh,
Across Death's gulf to us doth Poland pray :
    " Help, Frenchmen, help, ah, leave me not to die! "

THE OUTCAST.

So the world's at a loss to guess
　　How I come by my *De!* infers
I've, too, a craze for *vieille noblesse?*
　　I, noble? God forgive you, sirs!
I'm none of your nobility,
　　Ancient or any other style;
I love France—that's enough for me!
　　And for the rest, why, I'm *Canaille—*
　　　Canaille, sirs, rank *Canaille!*

Heav'n only knows why I should bear
　　This *De* you all so vastly prize!
For my poor sires enjoyed their share
　　Of a *grand seigneur's* tyrannies:
One of your real *grands seigneurs*, mind,
　　Who deigned to play the millstone, while
They were the grain for him to grind!
　　Noblesse? Lord love you, I'm *Canaille—*
　　　Canaille, sirs, rank *Canaille!*

My sires were no broad-acred lords
  With serfs to trample in the mud ;
No bravos they, whose lacquered swords
  Made merry with the peasants' blood !
They held not Freedom in disdain
  To fawn on Clovis for a smile,
Or kiss the hem of Pepin's train !
  Noblesse? Lord love you, I'm *Canaille—*
    Canaille, sirs, rank *Canaille!*

With fellow-countrymen for foes
  My fathers' spurs were never won,
They never hailed in France, God knows,
  The hated Arms of Albion !
Nor when the State to ruin's brink
  Was well-nigh brought by Priesthood's guile,
Were their pens steeped in Treason's ink.
  Noblesse? Lord love you, I'm *Canaille—*
    Canaille, sirs, rank *Canaille!*

Leave me, then, to my lowly rôle !
  Yes, you, who, snuffing Fortune's breeze,
Patricians of the button-hole,
  Worship each new sun on your knees.

I'm of the dregs ! but then, you see
(Cynics aren't after all so vile !),
I only flatter Poverty !
Noblesse? Lord love you, I'm *Canaille—*
Canaille, sirs, rank *Canaille !*

A BIRTHDAY LETTER.

(*From the King of Rome to the Duke of Bordeaux.*)

My heartiest greetings I send
  On your Highness's début in life;
Fortune figures no doubt as your friend,
  With the richest of promises rife!
So it was at the time of my birth;
  Kings crowded their homage to pay,
Round my cot cringed the lords of the earth—
  And yet I'm an exile to-day!

The minstrels who made me their theme,
  In you the same interest take;
At christening functions they seem
  As much in request as the cake!
For your baptism rite, I opine,
  The Seine will the water purvey;
They sent to the Jordan for mine—
  And yet I'm an exile to-day!

The same parasitical crowd
  That for you such a future foresees,
When I was their idol, avowed
  That the Lilies must yield to the Bees!

Ev'n the nurse in whose arms I was borne
    Had her servile patrician array
To proffer their homage each morn—
    And yet I'm an exile to-day!

With laurels my couch was laid out,
    You merely in purple recline ;
A rattle's your plaything, no doubt,
    A sceptre was wont to be mine !
For my cap I a crown was decreed ;
    From a Pontiff 'twas taken away,
While prelates applauded the deed—
    And yet I'm an exile to-day!

Your marshals, so braggartly brave,
    Will serve but your fortunes to foil ;
Base tinsel is all that they crave,
    From Honour's pure star they recoil !
To my sire they were bound by an oath
    He believed they could never betray;
All was staked on their oft-vaunted troth—
    And yet I'm an exile to-day !

Should yours ever grow a great name,
   When mine is forgotten on earth,
Put the time-serving traitors to shame
   By recalling the tale of my birth !
As their lies in your ear they outpour,
   Of your cousin remind them, and say :
" Thus also to him ye once swore,
   And yet he's an exile to-day ! "

THE COURT SUIT.

COME, mentors, to the right-about,
   I mean to go in spite of you!
Here, my good Moses, pick me out
   Your handsomest in gold and blue.
I've caught at last the royal eye,
   And, fairly launched in Fortune's race,
I'm off to wait on Majesty,
   And swell it in a suit of lace!

Ambition whispers in my ear,
   Already I can feel its glow—
Zounds, I shall come to grief, I fear,
   If I can't bow a shade more low—
Won't they just stare, the passers-by,
   To see how I can go the pace!
I'm off, sirs, to his Majesty!
   How do you like my suit of lace?

Being minus my barouche as yet,
   I start on foot, but on the way
By a *bon vivant* friend am met,
   Who hauls me off to *déjeûner*.

"Can't give you very long," said I,
"Or I shall get into disgrace,
Engaged, man, to his Majesty!
    Don't you observe my suit of lace?"

Scarce from the table had I stole
    When Master Benedict comes up,
Insisting, hospitable soul,
    That I should taste his loving-cup!
Gad! how the bottles seemed to fly!
    Already I'd discussed a brace,
When—how about his Majesty?
    And how about my suit of lace?

In spite of claret and champagne,
    Still to ambition's promptings true,
I bravely stagger off again
    To seek my royal interview.
But what should chance to meet my eye,
    Close to the gate, but Rose's face?
And Rose—well, she's a Majesty
    Who doesn't want a suit of lace!

Far from the Court where, sooth to say,
　Beauty is art, and **Love** a leer,
To Rose's room I haste away,
　Where none can see and none can hear.
And there my coat, I can't deny,
　Makes Rose first smile, and then grimace;
To the winds went his Majesty,
　And with him went my suit of lace!

And so my giddy dream is gone,
　I find myself myself once more;
My nightcap once again I don,
　And in my attic soundly snore!
And, gentle reader, by-the-bye,
　You'll please remember that in case
You want to wait on Majesty,
　You're welcome to my suit of lace!

HARLEQUIN.

(*A Funeral Oration.*)

He's gone : farewell to gaiety!
 He's gone : farewell to quips and cranks!
No more he'll cheer us with his glee,
 No more he'll charm us with his pranks!
His mirth and motley all the year
 Made every moment joyous spin;
Then, ah, a tear, a tear, a tear
 Upon the grave of Harlequin!

Our age so wonderfully wise,
 So well equipped with Learning's keys,
Ne'er dreamed that his fantastic guise
 Concealed a second Socrates!
Clio, unclasp your tablets bright,
 Fame everlasting let him win,
In golden letters write, write, write
 The history of Harlequin.

Tho' to a high-born abbess he
 His birth indubitably owed,
For his patrician pedigree
 No sort of reverence he showed.

The Bishop, too, his noble sire,
　He disavowed with shrug and grin ;
Ah, then admire, admire, admire
　The sound good sense of Harlequin !

With martial emulation fired,
　In early days a pike he bore,
But with a wound or two retired,
　To ply his craft from door to door.
With song to silence every sigh
　Was his receipt thro' thick and thin ;
Ah, if we all would try, try, try
　The panacea of Harlequin !

Cheerily scrubbing every morn
　His humble sabots thus he'd sing :
" Tho' Wealth my wooden shoes may scorn,
　They well are worth the polishing !
For where's the leather that would make
　A pair I'd trip so lightly in ? "
Ah, then a lesson take, take, take
　From philosophic Harlequin !

"Uncover for the King!" they'd cry;
  "With all my heart," he'd answer pat,
" If he'll take off his crown, while I
  Remove my ragamuffin hat!
Faith! if my head at all I bare,
  'Tis with the baker I'll begin!"—
Ah, well if all would share, share, share
  The honest pride of Harlequin!

"Why want," they'd hint, "for daily bread,
  When loyal songs command a fee?"
"Never," he'd cry, "shall it be said
  My stage encouraged Tyranny!"
"To prison then, away with you!"—
  "Who for your prisons cares a pin?"
To Freedom ever true, true, true,
  All his life long was Harlequin!

"D'you want a priest?"—"Parbleu, not I;
  Black coats were never in my line;
In opposite directions lie
  Their mummeries, you see, and mine!

Their creed I deem preposterous,
  Mine they pronounce a deadly sin !"—
Ah, well, for us, for us, for us,
  The simple faith of Harlequin !

Sirs, the good friend for whom we grieve
  Owned to one failing and but one ;
His mother was a child of Eve,
  And he was—well, his mother's son !
Of the forbidden apple he
  Ate every morsel, pip and skin !—
Ah, never, never, never, we
  Shall find the like of Harlequin !

FIFTY!

THESE flowers denote a fête? Ah, no,
  A fast they rather should portray!
For I've jogged thro' this world of woe
  Just half a century to-day!
Ah, how the years like lightning fly,
  Ah, how the hours unhallowed flit,
And then the crowsfoot round the eye!
  I'm fifty, and be hanged to it!

Yes, I'm the age when all's askew;
  Mildewed the fruit, and sere the tree.
A knock! ah, knock till all is blue,
  You'll get small change, sir, out of me!
Some scoundrel of a quack, I'll bet,
  Who snuffs an apoplectic fit;
Once I'd have sworn it was Lisette!
  I'm fifty, and be hanged to it!

O'er Age a thousand horrors creep;
  Now with the gout one's doomed to writhe,
Now blindness builds her dungeon deep,
  Or deafness makes our dear friends blithe;

Last, Reason's lamp, long faint of flame,
  Becomes to all intents unlit.
Youth, your respect we well may claim —
  I'm fifty, and be hanged to it !

Hark, I hear Death upon the road,
  Rubbing his grisly hands in glee ;
He's dug his ditch, awaits his load :
  " Make your farewells, my friend," snarls he.
Up there a blank sky at the best,
  Here famine, sword, and fever-pit ;
Well, it's about time for a rest—
  I'm fifty, and be hanged to it !

But stay, there's yet your twining arm,
  My worn heart's hand-maiden and nurse,
You who my brooding spirit charm
  Out of the dreams that are its curse ;
Ay, and the blossoms of your spring
  Keep for this brow by winter knit,
A very angel ministering !—
  I'm fifty, and a fig for it !

MY CHOICE.

DEAR daughter of the people, on me, the people's
   bard,
   The blossom of your Spring-tide you lavishly
      bestow,
And if you grudged the guerdon 'twould be a trifle
   hard,
   For with my earliest warbling I soothed your
      earliest woe !
Dream not that dames patrician my troth will e'er
   entice,
   Tho' robed in richest raiment, by proudest titles
      styled ;
My muse will bear me witness I boast but one
   device—
   The offspring of the people, for me the people's
      child !

When still a friendless stripling I trod Life's path
   unknown,
   And gazed upon the strongholds of opulence and
      pride,

Think not that tho' an outcast upon the wide world
   thrown,
   I envied them their splendour or for their riches
     sighed :
Ah no, methought, the glory for evermore has
   fled
   Those halls where song enchanted and chivalry
     beguiled,
Blot out their time-worn mottoes and write up this
   instead—
   The offspring of the people, for me the people's
     child !

Out on your gilded chambers where Pleasure only
   cloys,
   Drear haunts of hollow grandeur and luxury for-
     lorn,
Whose mirth is as the rocket which one brief shower
   destroys,
   Whose gladness an abortion that dies as soon as
     born !
In shoes that shun a carpet, straw hat, and cotton
   gown,
   Amid the laughing meadows you all the week
     run wild,

And every Sunday welcome your troubadour from
    town—
    The offspring of the people, for me the people's
        child !

Point out to me the beauty, princess or simple dame,
    Whose charm is more enchanting, whose grace is
        more complete ;
A heart so full of freshness not one of them could
    claim,
    An eye so archly tender, a countenance so sweet !
The tyrant-trampled people its mark at last has
    made,
    I braved for them two sceptres, and victory on me
        smiled,
With you and your devotion my prowess they've
    repaid—
    The offspring of the people, for me the people's
        child !

THE OLD CORPORAL.

FALL in there, comrades, to your places !
    Out with your swords, your muskets prime ;
I've got my pipe, had your embraces,
    And now for my discharge !—it's time.
My lads, don't you outlive your day,
    Or you'll keep me in countenance !—
Well, in the regiment I've grown grey !—
            Recruits, advance !
            No whimpering now.
            March, you know how,
        Recruits, eyes front ! quick march !

The colonel, lads, insulted me,
    I struck the coward back his lie ;
Well, by the code it's right, you see,
    And the old corporal must die ;
Maybe it was the liquor, or
    The devil made my old eyes dance—
Then I'd fought for the Emperor !

Recruits, advance !
No whimpering now.
March, you know how,
Recruits, eyes front ! quick march !

Recruits, brave deeds may cost too dear ;
  Sound limbs aren't after all bad things.
I won this cross that's fastened here,
  When we made nine-pins of the kings !
What drinks my fights have cost you, friends—
  But at such yarns best look askance,
For here's, you see, how glory ends !
    Recruits, advance !
    No whimpering now.
    March, you know how,
    Recruits, eyes front ! quick march !

You from my home there, you go back
  And take once more to minding sheep—
Look at those buds, they'll soon be black ;
  How fresh our spring-buds used to keep !

What armfuls of them, too, I'd get
   Before I clapped eyes on a lance !
God ! and my mother's living yet !—
     Recruits, advance !
       No whimpering now.
       March, you know how,
     Recruits, eyes front ! quick march !

Who's that there following us and crying ?
   Not our old sergeant's widow, eh ?
Ah, when that lad of hers seemed dying
   I carried him one livelong day.
They'd have joined Jacques beneath the snow
   Had it not been for me, perchance,
So I shall have her prayers, I know.
     Recruits, advance !
       No whimpering now.
       March, you know how,
     Recruits, eyes front ! quick march !

Sacre ! my pipe's out ; no, it's not ;
   Good, I shall waste a match the less.
Ah, to the Square so soon we've got ?—
   I shan't want any bandages.

My thanks, my lads, before I go.
   Get home again when you've the chance—
And for God's sake don't fire too low !
      Recruits, advance !
         No whimpering now.
         March, you know how,
      Recruits, eyes front ! quick march !

THE COURT CENSORS.

So, madame, it amuses you
   With Lise's morals to make free !
Ah well, she's a grisette, it's true
   (King Cupid's aristocracy !),
And with her coquetries a spell
   O'er half the Paris sparks has thrown !
Upon your charms she doesn't dwell,
   Then, leave her character alone !

O'er Dives you deride her sway,
   Yet ill can you afford to laugh,
Who every night in Jewry pay
   Your homage to the golden calf !
Since, too, for no illiberal fee
   You rallied round the Empire's throne,
When Lise attacks Legitimacy,
   Best leave her character alone !

Love, tho' inert for many a year,
   Luring old age one often sees ;
I know a certain saintly peer
   Who'll make a marchioness of Lise ;

Thanks to her arts and graces, he
  Will soon emerge a duke full-blown ;
Lise once *au mieux* with Royalty,
  You'll leave her character alone !

Converted by her coronet,
  You ladies, now so prompt to sneer,
Her antecedents will forget
  And freely at her fêtes appear !
But even splendour's apt to pall;
  So when some morning, pious grown,
She steals to the confessional,
  We'll leave her character alone !

Virtue, I'd have you understand,
  Is strangely various in its hue ;
Yours tallies with the titles grand,
  Your lacquey bawls in front of you !
They to the highest stilts resort
  Who most at heart to mud are prone—
Lise, if you ever go to Court,
  I'll—leave your character alone !

EPIGRAM.

(On sending some songs to a young lady.)

In these songs that I send are portrayed
  Two spells of dominion supreme,
Love, reduced in my case to a shade,
  And Glory, that fugitive dream !
As to Love, you ne'er knelt at his shrine,
  While Fame you incessantly woo ;
Yet Love I'm disposed to opine
  Is the safer to trust of the two !

THE GOD OF GOOD FOLK.

THERE is a God of whom my prayers,
 Poor as I am, no boon request ;
I watch the world and its affairs,
 Cherish the good, forget the rest ;
And Pleasure, howe'er priests may prate,
 My modest creed does not offend,
Gaily I drink, and leave my fate
  To God, the good folk's friend !

Beside my pillow Poverty
 Sits brooding, but I heed her not,
For thanks to Love and Hope, you see,
 I dream a bed of down my lot.
Mine no stern God that priests create,
 Gentle is he to whom I bend ;
Gaily I drink, and leave my fate
  To God, the good folk's friend !

A conquering despot drunk with power,
 Nations and dynasties down flings,
The dust his charger's proud hoofs shower
 Begrimes the sacred brows of kings.

Crawl on, crawl on, ye fallen great,
　What reck I how your glories end?
Gaily I drink, and leave my fate
　　　To God, the good folk's friend!

'Mid France's miracles of Art,
　Rare trophies won from Art's own land,
I've lived to see with burning heart
　Her vanquishers triumphant stand!
Ay, Albion wreak on us your hate,
　But tides can turn and fortunes mend;
Gaily I drink, and leave my fate
　　　To God, the good folk's friend!

Oh, our foreboding friend the priest,
　With all his prophecies of gloom!
On hell-fire how he loves to feast,
　The end of Time, the crack of doom!
Come, Cherubim, your cheeks inflate,
　In flame and thunder-cloud descend!
Gaily I drink, and leave my fate
　　　To God, the good folk's friend!

What, God a God of anger?   Pooh,
  He made all and loves all He made;
The wine he gives ; my dear friends, you ;
  Love which is His creating aid ;
The charms of all these dissipate
  The nightmares priests rejoice to send !
Gaily I drink, and leave my fate
      To God, the good folk's friend.

OLD AGE.

(To my Comrades.)

His finger, implacable Time
  On our brows is preparing to lay,
We have still something left of our prime,
  But it hasn't much longer to stay!
And yet at each step that we take
  There is always a flower to unfold;
If the best of Life's blessings we make,
  We shall never, my comrades, grow old!

In vain would we conjure up mirth
  With carol and wine and good cheer,
Of something there's somewhere a dearth,
  It isn't the same as last year!
But if to the end of our days
  We can quaver a song joyous-soul'd,
To Bacchus a bumper upraise,
  We shall never, my comrades, grow old!

If at sixty we seek Beauty's shrine
    With the ardour of wild twenty-two,
Our homage she'll doubtless decline,
    And pronounce us too *passé* to woo!
But if to Time's edict we bend,
    And instead of a suit overbold,
Tender only the troth of a friend,
    We shall never, my comrades, grow old!

Life's journey then let us pursue,
    By the light that good fellowship lends,
And when Age with his ills steals in view,
    We'll confront him together, my friends!
Together, unheeding the blast,
    Together, defying the cold,
Arm in arm, side by side to the last,
    We shall never, shall never grow old!

TO MY GODCHILD.

(On her christening-day.)

My godchild !   Why you should be so
  The devil only knows, or heaven !
You scream at me, that's all I know,—
  Not that I care, you're quite forgiven;
Besides I've brought no bonbons—trying
  In a godfather, I daresay;
But come, my little one, stop crying,
  I'll make you laugh instead some day !

Friendship confers on me the post ;
  Friendship bestows on you the name ;
I'm but a toiler, at the most,
  An honest toiler all the same.
If then on presents you're relying,
  Why, I have none to give away ;
But come, my little one, stop crying,
  I'll make you laugh instead some day !

Hard as the best of us may try,
   We prate but to perform the less ;
Still may your godmother and I
   Add something to your happiness !
Tho' here be sobbing, there be sighing,
   A good heart nothing need dismay ;
So then, my little one, stop crying,
   I'll make you laugh instead some day !

Yes, for your wedding-song I'll sing,
   If by that time my song still flows,
And I'm not also sojourning
   Where Collé and Panard repose ;
But what, in shade and silence lying,
   While you're the gayest of the gay ?
No, no, my little one, stop crying,
   I'll make you laugh instead some day !

MY FINE.

Ten thousand francs, I'm fined ten thousand francs!
  A handsome premium for a prison cell
From one who's passed his days in Penury's ranks,
  And dines on crusts indifferently well!
Come, can't your Lordship say a trifle less?
  "No no, your ribald pen's too long had sway,
His Majesty at least must have redress,
  So in his name ten thousand francs you pay!"

Well, I submit; but how d'you mean to spend
  This cash with which I hoped to make so free?
In hiring help from some more learned friend,
  Or on the prosecuting Counsel's fee?
Whose greasy purse gapes yonder to be lined?
  The spy's, whose bill you've promised to defray?
He's sworn that I pollute the public mind;
  Two thousand francs to perjury we'll pay!

Yes, by your leave I'll parcel out my fine,
  I've got no end of applicants enrolled!
What's that beneath the throne? Ye muses nine,
  A harp! Have all the palace bards caught cold?

Sing, my fine fellows, and requite your muse
   By grabbing everything that comes your way,
(Tho', for God's sake, don't smash the Holy
     Cruse !)—
Two thousand francs to flummery we'll pay !

Whom have we next? A heterogeneous crew
   Of Brobdignagian nobles grandly starr'd !
Some pedigreed from Pepin, some more new,
   But all with toadyism's brush well tarr'd !
A goodly slice from Fortune's cake they cut ;
   Why not? Aren't they Brobdignags, who some
     day
To their own height will raise poor Lilliput ?—
   Two thousand francs to flunkeydom we'll pay !

Now for copes, croziers, gold and silver plate,
   Coats of arms, mitres, red-hats, retinues,
Palaces, abbeys, semi-regal state—
   The Cloth's a desperate stickler for its dues !
One of their saintships, shocked at what I sing,
   Has doomed me to the nether depths, they say !
Already my good angel's singed her wing !—
   Three thousand francs to godliness we'll pay !

And now for the grand total !   Two and two
   Make four, and three make seven, and three make
      ten !—
La Fontaine wasn't fined a single sou,
   But times, you see, were somewhat different then !
Louis was too magnanimous to treat
   A poor bard so for just a pungent lay !—
Come, Mr. Tipstaff, make out your receipt ;
   I'll pay, long live his Majesty, I'll pay !

THE WHIPPER-SNAPPERS.

BEING somewhat prone to sorcery,
  A soothsayer I lately sought,
Who in a glass revealed to me
  The boundless future, quick as thought !
And, O ye Gods, just think of it,
  France, tho' a century had flown,
In one thing hadn't changed a bit !—
  The " Barbons " still were on the throne !

Our race had into dwarfs declined,
  Had come, in fact, to such a pass
That they can only be defined
  As midges on the magic glass !
France scarce the shadow seemed to be
  Of the great France I once had known,
So dwindled was her sovereignty !—
  The " Barbons " still were on the throne !

What imps infinitesimal !
  Jesuits barely two foot six !
Priests preternaturally small,
  Each with an elfin crucifix !

All whom they blessed were brought to doom,
   Even the old French Court had grown
Into a petty pupil-room!—
   The "Barbons" still were on the throne!

All pigmy! palace, magazine,
   Trade, science, education, art!
Not seldom, too, upon the scene
   Gay little famines played their part!
While in the lines of Lilliput,
   To penny trumpets proudly blown,
A little army tried to strut!—
   The "Barbons" still were on the throne!

At length upon the horoscope,
   As climax to this vision drear,
A giant seemed to interlope,
   Half shadowing the hemisphere;
And as their little speeches pat
   The mannikins prepared to drone,
He popped them all into his hat!—
   The "Barbons" still were on the throne!

THE CROWN.

(A Twelfth-Night Song.)

AND so the cake declares me king !
  Come, subjects, crown me on the spot !
Don't spare the bottle, have your fling,
  And envy me my royal lot !
What soul is there that isn't bent
  Some time or other on renown ?
Who with his hat would be content,
  Could he exchange it for a crown ?

The crown that cumbers Cæsar's brow,
  Rubies and diamonds begem ;
Jacques claims his kingdom thro' the plough,
  And hedge-flowers are his diadem !
Pomp for the circlet has to pay,
  Love gives it gratis to the clown ;
Cæsar at night waves his away,
  Jacques sleeps the sounder for his crown !

9

The sons of France, with sword and song,
  To France a double glory bring ;
To them the laurels twice belong,
  They conquer and of conquest sing !
If Mars his favour should refuse,
  And Fortune's smile become a frown,
Haply their sceptre they may lose,
  But never will they lose their crown !

Coy sylph, as yet content to wear
  The crown that innocence bestows,
Courtiers already crowd your stair
  With arts that lure and lips that gloze ;
Too soon they'll throng to bend the knee
  And kiss the border of your gown ;
You'll listen to their flattery,
  And some fine morning—lose your crown !

But, lose a crown ? Ah, that warns me
  I'd better take good care of mine !
Well, I'm no tax-eater, you see,
  And boast no prehistoric line,

So, subjects, brim your bumpers gay,
  I've not a single dread to drown,
And till dessert's done, any way,
  Don't make me abdicate my crown !

THE NIGHTINGALE.

SLEEP reigns o'er the city once more,
    Not a soul is astir in the street;
From afar, beloved nightingale, pour
    Thy strain so entrancingly sweet !
'Tis the moment when back to her sway
    Soft Reverie hastens to wing,
'Tis the hour of all hours in the day,
    Then sing to me, nightingale, sing !

Thou tellest of love that is strong,
    And steadfast and tender and pure,
Then lift not to Phryne thy song,
    Whose love is a feint and a lure !
Whose smiles are the smiles of the mart,
    Whose honey envelops a sting—
My love, 'tis the love of the heart,
    Then sing to me, nightingale, sing !

The miser who lives but to gloat
    O'er the sight of his treasures untold,
Not thy richest, most rapturous note
    One moment will wean from his gold !

How he shivers and shakes in his shoes
  At the thought of what midnight may bring!
I'm poor, so can sport with the muse,
  Then sing to me, nightingale, sing !

The courtier who year after year
  His fetters is willing to wear,
Is he worthy one accent to hear
  Of your rhapsody free as the air ?
A minion ! contented to be
  At the beck and the call of a king !
When *I* bow, 'tis to Freedom, you see,
  Then sing to me, nightingale, sing !

Your song into ecstasy grows,
  With the base you can never have part !
Nature's voice thro' your utterance flows,
  Each note brings her nearer my heart !
Each note wakes a dream of delight,
  A perfume, a transport of spring !—
Till morning again glistens bright,
  Ah, sing to me, nightingale, sing !

THE COSSACK'S SONG.

My glorious steed, the Cossack's pride, the Cossack's one ally,
The war-trump of the North resounds, off like the
north wind fly!
I scent the slain for plunder heaped, I snuff the
cannon's breath,
Once more shall Death thy rider be, those hoofs
the wings of Death!
Thy stately crest no ribands crown, thy saddle-
cloth is bare,
Wait only for the battle's wreck, and thou shalt
have thy share!
Hark to that neigh's fierce clarion, see how the
foam he flings,
He tramples nations in his stride, and plants his
hoof on kings!

Peace, who too long has toyed with it, to me thy
    rein has tost,
The ancient landmarks of the West for evermore
    are lost.
Again I see the jewels gleam, again I clutch the
    gold—
Off to the land of palaces we scoured so well of old!
The waters of the rebel Seine, as twice they've
    done before,
Shall slake thy thirst, thou noble one, and cleanse
    thy flanks of gore!
Hark to that neigh's fierce clarion, see how the
    foam he flings,
He tramples nations in his stride, and plants his
    hoof on kings!

Priests, nobles, princes, emperors, all huddled in
    one tuck,
Cowering at last beneath the blow for centuries
    unstruck,
Wail out from their captivity, "Come, crush us at
    thy will,
We'll brook thy harshest tyrannies but to be tyrants
    still!"

I go to their deliverance, I give them their desire,
Before my lance their Cross shall crouch, their
    sceptres sweep the mire !
Hark to that neigh's fierce clarion, see how the
    foam he flings,
He tramples nations in his stride, and plants his
    hoof on kings !

Once in my lonely bivouac I saw a phantom loom,
A phantom of majestic form, whose dread eye
    pierced the gloom.
" Once more," it cried, "my sovereignty rears its
    immortal crest ! "
Then with its shadowy battle-axe it pointed towards
    the West.
'Twas the great son of Attila, whose shade walks
    to this day,
The mighty monarch of the Huns ; his bidding I
    obey !
Hark to that neigh's fierce clarion, see how the
    foam he flings,
He tramples nations in his stride, and plants his
    hoof on kings !

That pyramid of glory which has turned proud
    Europe's brain,
That armoury of knowledge she has called upon
    in vain,
Once I leap into that saddle, once I give that rein
    a shake,
Will be even as the sand-grains thou wilt scatter
    in thy wake !
Court, palace, temple, treasure, law, tradition,
    custom, creed,
All shall vanish, and for ever, in the whirlwind of
    thy speed !
Hark to that neigh's fierce clarion, see how the
    foam he flings,
He tramples nations in his stride, and plants his
    hoof on kings !

A METAMORPHOSIS.

WHAT, madam, *you* Lisette !
You with your fine toilette,
Your fashionable curls,
Your diamonds and pearls !
No, no, you're not Lisette,
She was a gay grisette !
    To bear that name
    You've lost all claim,
No, no, you're not Lisette !

Your feet, in satin shod,
Shrink from the vulgar sod ;
Your cheeks with bloom abound ;
How much is it a pound ?
No, no, you're not Lisette,
She was a gay grisette !
    To bear that name
    You've lost all claim,
No, no, you're not Lisette !

With gauds of every kind
Your boudoir's grandly lined ;
Even your very bed
Is ormolu, 'tis said !
No, no, you're not Lisette,
She was a gay grisette !
 To bear that name
 You've lost all claim,
No, no, you're not Lisette !

Your smile, so arch of old,
Has grown superbly cold ;
Jests you consider low,
You're now a wit, you know !
No, no, you're not Lisette,
She was a gay grisette !
 To bear that name
 You've lost all claim,
No, no, you're not Lisette !

Ah, for the days gone by,
When, throned six storeys high,
Love's empress, you were fain
In calico to reign !

No, no, you're not Lisette,
She was a gay grisette !
  To bear that name
  You've lost all claim,
No, no, you're not Lisette !

Your sprightly glances then
Would witch a dozen men,
And yet you weren't somehow,
Well—not what you are now !
No, no, you're not Lisette,
She was a gay grisette !
  To bear that name
  You've lost all claim,
No, no, you're not Lisette !

Yet, why my venom vent ?
You're after all content ;
In jewels, dinners, dress,
You've found your happiness !
No, no, you're not Lisette,
She was a gay grisette !
  To bear that name
  You've lost all claim,
No, no, you're not Lisette !

Well, *chacun a sor goût !*
I'm much too low for you,
For me you're far too high,
So—to your Grace good-bye !
No, no, you're not Lisette,
She was a gay grisette !
    To bear that name
    You've lost all claim,
No, no, you're not Lisette !

MY CALLING.

TUMBLED upon the world
    An ugly wretched wight,
Here buffeted, there hurled,
    Mankind against a mite,
When oft my misery
    A plaintive moan would wring,
The good God said to me,
    " Sing, poor little one, sing ! "

By rich, and proud, and great
    Down-ridden, overborne;
Now cowering 'neath their hate,
    Now writhing 'neath their scorn,
No matter where I flee
    Their insults still they fling !
The good God says to me,
    " Sing, poor little one, sing ! "

Filled ever with the dread
    Of starving, a lone waif,
To earn my dole of bread
    'Neath Labour's chain I chafe ;

As, pining to be free,
  I stave off Hunger's sting,
The good God says to me,
  "Sing, poor little one, sing!"

In pity for my woes
  Love soothed me for awhile,
But with Youth's waning rose
  He too has ceased to smile ;
As Beauty spurns my plea,
  And wayward Love takes wing,
The good God says to me,
  "Sing, poor little one, sing!"

To sing (be sure I'm right!),
  To sing God sent me here,
And those my songs delight,
  To them at least I'm dear!
When the wine circles free,
  And fêtes their frolics bring,
The good God says to me,
  "Sing, poor little one, sing!"

THE WISEACRE.

My excellent friends, I've a sermon to give,
  So pass round the wine and my homily heed ;
In freedom and ease let us all of us live,
  Whatever your destiny, stick to that creed !
Make pastime your object, and pleasure and glee;
  From grandeur and riches turn frowning away—
Such, at least, is the precept propounded by me,
  Whose hair with sheer wisdom is fast growing
    grey !

My excellent friends, if you have a spare hour,
  And are willing to spend it in frolic and mirth,
Don't disdain jolly Bacchus, whose magic has power
  To dispel all the cares that encumber the earth !
One sip from his beaker, whate'er the brand be,
  Makes the gloomiest heart in the universe gay—
Such, at least, is the precept propounded by me,
  Whose hair with sheer wisdom is fast growing
    grey !

My excellent friends, what are laughter and wine
  If Love lend not also his infinite charms?
Then bask in the glances of Beauty divine,
  And spend every moment you can in her arms!
Her gifts far excel, as we all must agree,
  The choicest that Glory and Wealth can array—
Such, at least, is the precept propounded by me,
  Whose hair with sheer wisdom is fast growing
    grey!

My excellent friends, it is thus we defeat
  The deadliest ills that Misfortune can shower;
So feast on Life's honey while yet it is sweet,
  Too long left untasted 'twill only turn sour!
While young, with the good things before you make
    free,
  Time enough when you're doting the piper to
    pay—
Such, at least, is the precept propounded by me,
  Whose hair with sheer wisdom is fast growing
    grey!

THE REFUSAL.

(Addressed to General Sebastiani.)

A MINISTER offers me gold !
Not a creature, of course, to be told,
    Not a word to appear in the press !
My wants are but few, to be sure,
And yet, when I think of the poor,
    I long to be rich, I confess !

With the poor, as the world is aware,
Stars and ribands one cannot well share,
    But gold is a different thing !
Yes, just for a hundred francs down,
I'd cheerfully pawn both my crown
    And my sceptre, if I were a king !

When money does come in my way,
It goes the next moment astray,
    How and where I can't really explain ;

My pocket is cursed with a hole
Which my grandmother, excellent soul,
　　All her days would have stitched at in vain!

All the same, my good friend, keep your gold!
In my teens, if the truth must be told,
　　Proud Freedom I fervently woo'd ;
Yes, I, who have vaunted in song
Lax loveliness all my life long,
　　Am wedded in fact to a prude !

Ay, Liberty, Sir, you must learn,
Is a bigot inflexibly stern,
　　Who, heedless of time and of place,
Directly the tinsel she spies
On Servility's livery, cries,
　　" Away with that rascally lace ! "

Your dross she an insult would deem !
But, frankly, how came you to dream
　　Of attempting to treat with *my* muse?
As it is, I'm at least a good " sou,"
But lacquer me over, and you
　　Make me counterfeit ev'n among "sous."

Keep your pelf ; I'm no hero, I fear,
But if the world happens to hear
　　Of this secret you think so profound,
You'll know whence the story has sprung—
My heart's like a lyre newly strung,
　　One touch, and you make it resound !

MY REPUBLIC.

I'VE got Republics on the brain,
  Now that I've seen so much of kings,
Have one, in fact, myself in train,
  Of which I mean to pull the strings !
Its only commerce shall be wine,
  Its only code a jest-book be,
Its only business well to dine,
  Its only motto, Liberty !

Come, my dear friends, your glasses fill !
  The Chambers are convoked to-day,
And for a first decree we will
  On *ennui* our proscription lay—
But stop, "proscription"?—I taboo
  That word in regions ruled by me,
With *ennui* what have we to do ?
  Pleasure alone crowns Liberty !

Enjoyment and luxuriousness
  We'll unrelentingly divorce ;
Fetters no more shall Thought repress,
  Bacchus shall put that law in force !

Unchallenged every creed shall pass,
  And every worshipper go free ;
Ay, you may even go to Mass :—
  So it's laid down by Liberty !

Nobility's too insolent,
  War then on titles we'll proclaim ;
The best of us shall ne'er consent
  To tack a handle to his name ;
And should a renegade dare pine
  For crown and sceptre, why, sirs, he
Shall have his cravings cooled in wine !
  We'll have no tricks with Liberty !

To our Republic then we'll drink !
  May it eternally endure !—
But stop, I'm half inclined to think
  It's not so perfectly secure !
Love's empire snares us in its net !
  Once more we humbly bend the knee,
And kiss—the white hand of Lisette !—
  Zooks ! it's all up with Liberty !

THE OLD SINGER.

FRIENDS, I heard you singing, so
  Crept amid your merry throng,
For I'm too a singer, though
  All but ended in my song !
Ah, what revelries were mine
  With the gallant and the gay !—
Friends of Woman, Glory, Wine,
  Frown not on my faltering lay !

What ! you toast me with a cheer,
  Welcome beaming in your eyes?
Who could such a greeting hear
  And not feel his spirits rise?
Revel while the roses twine,
  Time to stop when leaves turn grey !—
Friends of Woman, Glory, Wine,
  Frown not on my faltering lay !

Once I had my loves like you
    (As your grandmothers will own !),
Comrades, ay, and riches too—
    Comrades, riches, all are flown !
Ah, how oft at Memory's shrine
    Have I mused upon that day !—
Friends of Woman, Glory, Wine,
    Frown not on my faltering lay !

Wrecked for France on Fortune's sea,
    True to her I've held thro' all !
In the few sips left to me
    There's no single drop of gall !
Ev'n I sang as from my vine
    Others filched the fruit away !—
Friends of Woman, Glory, Wine,
    Frown not on my faltering lay !

Albeit veteran of a field
    Which your valour never knew,
All its trophies would I yield
    Just for once to march with you !

In your watchword I divine
  Promise of a nobler fray !—
Friends of Woman, Glory, Wine,
  Frown not on my faltering lay !

Ah, the future *you* will rear ! —
  Comrades ! one last toast I crave,
" Freedom ! may she reappear
  With her glow to gild my grave ! "
Then, from where your sunbeams shine
  I will pass upon my way.—
Friends of Woman, Glory, Wine,
  Frown not on my faltering lay !

MY INDEPENDENCE.

My independence venerate,
    Ye slaves to Fashion bound !
'Twas not among the rich and great
    That Liberty I found !
My songs have pretty plainly shown
    The charm she has for me !—
Lisette may laugh, and she alone,
    When I declare I'm free !
When I declare I'm free as air,
    When I declare I'm free !

Yes, I'm a vagrant rough and rude
    Upon the face of earth,
Who battle against servitude,
    Armed with the sling of mirth !
Satire provides me with the stone,
    No bad one you'll agree !—
Lisette may laugh, and she alone,
    When I declare I'm free ! .
When I declare I'm free as air,
    When I declare I'm free !

Those parasites we laugh to scorn,
  Who to a sceptre cling,
From morn to night and night to morn,
  The creatures of a king !
Out on the bard who hymns a throne,
  And takes a tyrant's fee !—
Lisette may laugh, and she alone,
  When I declare I'm free !
When I declare I'm free as air,
  When I declare I'm free !

How soon mere power begins to pall !
  God help your royal wight !
The very victims of his thrall
  Can boast a better plight.
With Love I'd sooner share a bone,
  Than reign from sea to sea !—
Lisette may laugh, and she alone,
  When I declare I'm free !
When I declare I'm free as air,
  When I declare I'm free !

Contentedly my lowly lot
  I every morning greet,

A Crœsus, so a crust I've got,
  With Hope to make it sweet !
Ev'n if my pillow were a stone,
  Sound would my slumbers be !—
Lisette may laugh, and she alone,
  When I declare I'm free !
When I declare I'm free as air,
  When I declare I'm free !

But what ! Lisette, with all her charms
  And fascinations rife,
Waiting to lock me in her arms,
  A captive there for life !
No, no ! aren't empires thus o'erthrown ?
  Lisette, your lures I flee !
If you'd still laugh, leave well alone,
  And let me still be free !
Ay, free as air, my temptress fair,
  Free, free, for ever free !

A FORECAST.

FRIENDS, in me behold a seer !
In my horoscope shines clear
Everything as it will be
In the year of years A.D. !

No more bards with lying lays,
Bigwigs shudder at their praise ;
Courtiers scorn to scrape the knee,
In the year of years A.D. !

Played-out dice and "cent. per cent.,"
Noble lord, and city gent ;
Snobs the pink of chivalry,
In the year of years A.D. !

Friendship (in these days so fast !)
Warranted for life to last,
Unimpaired by Penury,
In the year of years A.D. !

Maidens in their teens demure,
In their twenties just as pure !
No pranks with Propriety,
In the year of years A.D. !

Wives on finery shall frown,
Husbands, called away from town,
Not return uneasily
In the year of years A.D. !

In whatever shall be writ
More real genius, less sham wit,
No sentimentality,
In the year of years A.D. !

Authors shall display more pride,
Actors own a world outside,
Critics learn civility,
In the year of years A.D. !

Grandeur's foibles shan't escape,
Nor the imps who grandeur ape;
Satire shall for once strike free
In the year of years A.D. !

Ton, in short, we shall regain,
Justice everywhere shall reign,
Truth break her captivity,
In the year of years A.D. !

Then, to Providence all praise,
Who our erring race will raise
To infallibility,
In the year of years A.D. !

THE PEOPLE'S ORPHEUS.

(An Elegy on Émile Debraux.)

HIS song is silenced in the tomb !
    Ah, where shall we his fellow find,
Whose ditties were as dainty bloom,
    Wafted upon a summer wind?
Of hurdy-gurdy and of fife,
    In every purlieu of the Poor,
His muse for years had been the life—
    He was the People's troubadour !

In Pleasure's beams he loved to bask,
    Mirth with a child's light heart adored ;
Like wine that gushes from a cask
    His life he laughingly outpoured ;
Pretentious Pomp he made his sport,
    To purse-proud Grandeur scorned to bend,
The " Quartier Latin " was his Court—
    Well was he called the People's friend !

" And did his poems bring him pay?"
   Sirs, not the shadow of a groat ;
Christmas that found you feasting gay
   Found him with tatters in his coat !
The north wind howls, his hearth is bare,
   Jack Frost thro' every crevice peers,
'Tis hailing here, 'tis snowing there—
   He sings to dry the People's tears !

We count the tears of kings, but who
   Shall number those the People shed ?
When all our laurels turned to rue,
   And Victory like a phantom fled ;
In every alley, every lane,
   'Mid lowliest lives, 'mid humblest lots,
His lyre awoke an answering strain—
   He made the People patriots !

He, in his Spring, has sped away,
   I, in my Winter, follow fast.
Ev'n as I weep a carol gay
   Borne from afar comes floating past ;

'Tis his !   The song those revellers sing
  Their sons shall echo by-and-by !
In the wide world is there a king
  The People thus would glorify?

Ah, then, to those he loved extend,
  Ye Rich and Great, a generous hand !
Of all except itself the friend,
  His genius struck on Penury's strand.
Grudge not your guerdon ; strains like his
  Half make the Poor forget their wrongs,
And tame them to your tyrannies !—
  The People's solace is their songs !

MY SHALLOP.

(Composed for my Birthday.)

By tranquil breezes, night and morn,
  Along a tranquil tide,
My little bark is lightly borne,
  Wherever Fate may guide.
With swelling sail she wings away !
  Afar, afar we float !
(Sweet zephyr, softly round her play !)
  On, on, my little boat !
With Fortune's wind a port we'll find,
  On, on, my little boat !

For fellow-passenger I take
  The muse of sprightly song ;
If only she will merry make,
  The voyage cannot be long !
Blither and blither grows her lay,
  Each happy mile we float !
(Sweet zephyr, softly round her play !)
  On, on, my little boat !

With Fortune's wind a port we'll find,
  On, on, my little boat !

What reck we if on yonder shore
  A tempest rages high,
Affrighting nations with its roar
  And making monarchs fly !
Pursuing still our placid way
  To Pleasure's bank we float !
(Sweet zephyr, softly round her play !)
  On, on, my little boat !
With Fortune's wind a port we'll find,
  On, on, my little boat !

Beneath those summer-tinted skies,
  Bathed in the summer-shine,
On yonder trellised hill-slope lies
  The empire of the vine !
There, nectar lurks in every spray,
  Then, thither let us float !
(Sweet zephyr, softly round her play !)
  On, on, my little boat !
With Fortune's wind a port we'll find,
  On, on, my little boat !

But see, what fairy fields are these
   I seem so well to know?
Whence yonder sylphs that thro' the trees
   In half-veiled beauty glow?
'Tis here that Love holds sovereign sway,
   Then, Love-wards let us float!
(Sweet zephyr, softly round her play!)
   On, on, my little boat!
With Fortune's wind a port we'll find,
   On, on, my little boat!

Past yonder rock that looms ahead,
   Begirt with laurel sere,
By a benignant planet led,
   For Friendship's cot we'll steer;
To mingle with her revels gay,
   Ah, swiftly let us float!
(Sweet zephyr, softly round her play!)
   On, on, my little boat!
With Fortune's wind a port we'll find,
   On, on, my little boat!

BOUQUET.

*(Presented to a Lady of Seventy on the day of
St. Marguerite.)*

A TRUCE to modern melody,
    Our friend is of the good old time!
Then, simple let the measure be,
    And wedded to the simplest rhyme!
Our modern music may be sweet,
    But there's a discord in its strains ;
With fine-drawn fancy and conceit,
        'Tis just a thought
        Too highly wrought !
Then, let us wake for Marguerite
    The old-world airs and gay refrains !

She in her youth was wont to trill
    The ditties of that golden day,
When Favart's love-chords quivered still,
    And Panard's satire still had sway !
Where could we now, I wonder, meet,
    For all our countless ills and banes,

With such an antidote complete,
    Of wit and glee
    And raillery?
Then, let us wake for Marguerite
  Those old-world airs and gay refrains!

By Memory's light how sweet to see
  The Past in all its brightness clad!
Song is a nation's history,
  Then surely Song should not be sad!
Time faster every hour will fleet;
  We'll make the most of what remains,
And humbly of the Gods entreat
    To let us sup
    Of Pleasure's cup,
That we may sing for Marguerite
  Full thirty years of gay refrains!

Then at the end, with glass in hand,
  White with the snows that Time has shed,
Around the table we will stand,
  And conjure Memory from the dead!
How every veteran heart will beat,
  As, Bacchus glowing in our veins,

We celebrate, till night's retreat
And daybreak peers,
The hundred years,
The hundred years of Marguerite
With old-world airs and gay refrains!

THE OLD FIDDLER.

I'M only an old fiddler, sirs,
Who scrapes to please the villagers,
       When summer eves are fine.
A wiseacre some worthies think ;
Wise enough, any way, to drink
       No water with my wine !
Come, lads and lasses, work is o'er,
Make merry in the shade once more !
Eh, tral-lal-la ! good village folk,
'Tis time to dance beneath my oak !

My dear old oak ! beneath its boughs
How many a Bacchanal carouse
       Its festive course has run !
However bitter they might be,
Here from all feud and rivalry
       Was rest for every one ;

And, ah, the courtships that its leaves
Have listened to in bygone eves !
Eh, tral-lal-la ! good village folk,
'Tis time to dance beneath my oak !

The master of yon moated pile
May well command your pitying smile,
    Although a lord of earth ;
In spite of all his power and pomp,
Be sure that as you gaily romp,
    He envies you your mirth !
And so when sulking in his coach
You see his mightiness approach,
Eh, tral-lal-la ! good village folk,
Dance, dance away beneath my oak !

Instead of venting pious hate
Upon the unregenerate,
    Heav'n in your prayers entreat
With plenteous grass his fields to bless,
To give his vineyards fruitfulness,
    And smile upon his wheat !
While if on Pleasure he be bent,
I'll sanctify his merriment !

Eh, tral-lal-la ! good village folk,
'Tis time to dance beneath my oak !

If, when you get your harvest in,
The hedge of quickset should be thin,
    That shields your neighbour's land,
Forbear to thrust your sickle thro'
And reap what was not sown by you,
    With surreptitious hand ;
No ! all such cravings to repress,
And keep your own in happiness,
Eh, tral-lal-la ! good village folk,
Come gaily dance beneath my oak !

When from the miseries of war
We wake to joyousness once more,
    And Peace resumes her sway,
Should those who for your sakes have bled
Seek shelter and a crust of bread,
    Ah, turn them not away !
No ! when the hurricane is past,
Succour the victims of the blast.
Eh, tral-lal-la ! good village folk,
'Tis time to dance beneath my oak !

Then, to my homilies give heed,
And gather round me, as I plead
    For Poverty and Woe ;
Praying that Enmity may cease,
And with the light of Love and Peace
    That every heart may glow !
Thus, for all time our green might be
An Eden of tranquillity !
Eh, tral-lal-la ! good village folk,
'Tis time to dance beneath my oak !

FIFTY CROWNS!

THE Gods be praised, I'm poor no more!
  Henceforth, my friends, consider me
  A gentleman of property;
My days of bread and scrape are o'er!
  Farewell to Fortune's flouts and frowns!
  I've fifty crowns, I've fifty crowns!
        Yes, every year
        I pocket clear
  A revenue of fifty crowns!

Comrades, the universe is mine!
  I could, if so I chose, maintain
  The splendour of a sovereign,
And with a hundred orders shine!
  Farewell to Fortune's flouts and frowns!
  I've fifty crowns, I've fifty crowns!
        Yes, every year
        I pocket clear
  A revenue of fifty crowns!

Wealth has its rights; without delay
  Mine shall be rigidly enforced,
  And in a carriage, nobly horsed,
I'll wish my creditors good-day !
    Farewell to Fortune's flouts and frowns !
    I've fifty crowns, I've fifty crowns !
        Yes, every year
        I pocket clear
    A revenue of fifty crowns !

Out on your wines of low degree !
  With oceans of the best Bordeaux
  My cellars shall henceforward flow,
Ay, and the finest Sillery!
    Farewell to Fortune's flouts and frowns !
    I've fifty crowns, I've fifty crowns !
        Yes, every year
        I pocket clear
    A revenue of fifty crowns !

Lise, if my favours you'd retain,
  You'll have to get up *à la mode*,
  Be fashionably furbelowed,
And never wear that print again !

Farewell to Fortune's flouts and frowns !
I've fifty crowns, I've fifty crowns !
　　Yes, every year
　　I pocket clear
A revenue of fifty crowns !

My roof shall never want a guest ;
　Relations, friends, of every hue,
　Par excellence, my comrades, you,
All shall be fêted on the best !
　Farewell to Fortune's flouts and frowns !
　I've fifty crowns, I've fifty crowns !
　　　Yes, every year
　　　I pocket clear
　A revenue of fifty crowns !

In fine, I mean to have my fling,
　And for a whole Elysian week
　On every sort of fun and freak
Squander my money like a king !
　Farewell to Fortune's flouts and frowns !
　I've fifty crowns, I've fifty crowns !
　　　Yes, every year
　　　I pocket clear
　A revenue of fifty crowns !

A THANKSGIVING.

At font and altar once I've stood
  To twenty times beside a grave ;
Yet many a heart by misery woo'd
  I've from itself contrived to save.
Dear God, thou hast been good to me ;
  I trip to-day, I fall to-morrow,
And yet can boast a gaiety
  That ne'er was known to jar on sorrow.

MY FAREWELL.

LAST night as, pen in hand, I mused intent,
 Trying to renovate my song-wreath's bloom,
Suddenly o'er my chair the fairy bent
 Who'd blessed me in the good old tailor's room ;
"Winter," she said, "has got you in his grip,
 'Tis time you took to dozing by the fire,
And ceased to fret with trembling finger-tip
 Your woe-begone and weather-beaten lyre ! "
Farewell, my songs, farewell ! the storm is o'er,
The bird that sang thro' it will sing no more !

"Perished the days," pursued she, "when your soul
 Seemed a perennial fountain-head of song,
When a bright meteor breaking all control,
 Your mirth flashed Life's dark firmament along ;
Ah me, how sadly changed the scene to-day,
 No single gleam illumes the horizon wan,
Not one remains of all your comrades gay,
 Even Lisette, the sweet Lisette, is gone ! "
Farewell, my songs, farewell ! the storm is o'er,
The bird that sang thro' it will sing no more !

"Yet murmur not, for thro' your voice the muse
   Has moved the lowliest of a mighty race ;
The humblest ear its highest accent woos,
   In the most ignorant heart it finds a place !
Only the few can oratory reach ;
   You, treating all creation as one choir,
True to the democratic creed you teach,
   Have linked the hurdy-gurdy to the lyre !"
Farewell, my songs, farewell ! the storm is o'er,
The bird that sang thro' it will sing no more !

"The shafts you launched against Oppression's
      throne
   Had hardly in the dust an instant lain,
Ere by the legions who your guidance own
   They were upgathered and sped on again !
Then, when its gauntlet Tyranny hurled down,
   Only at Freedom's first retort to fly,
Of all the shots that struck the caitiff crown,
   Did not your muse the deadliest supply ?"
Farewell, my songs, farewell ! the storm is o'er,
The bird that sang thro' it will sing no more !

"Proud was the part that in those days you played,
   Never so much as dreaming of reward,

And with their golden memory shall the shade
   Of your fast-falling eventide be stored !
To the brave sons of France a beacon be,
   Shine o'er their vessel, every quicksand show :
And when at last she rides in Victory,
   Sun your pale spirit in her glory's glow !"
Farewell, my songs, farewell ! the storm is o'er,
The bird that sang thro' it will sing no more !

Dear Fairy, humbly doing your behest,
   To Fame the jaded minstrel makes his bow ;
Oblivion (cause and consequence of rest !),
   Oblivion's all that I can look for now ;
Yet haply when I sink into the tomb,
   Some old survivor of the fight will say,
" Once gloriously his star shone thro' the gloom,
   Tho' dimmed by Heav'n long ere 'twas lost for
      aye ! "
Farewell, my songs, farewell ! the storm is o'er,
The bird that sang thro' it will sing no more !

NOTES.

---◆---

The Boxers (p. 38).—This song was written during the occupation of Paris by the Allies, a period in which English influence and English visitors largely predominated.

Poland (p. 43).—This song, in which Béranger seems to reach his highest note, was published, together with "Poniatowski" and "A mes amis devenus ministres" (To my friends become ministers), in 1831 for the benefit of the Polish Committee.

Good-Night! (p. 53).—This song was dedicated to his old friend M. Laisney, a printer, to whom Béranger was apprenticed in his early days. M. Laisney, himself a dabbler in verse, encouraged and aided Béranger in his first literary efforts.

The Grandmother's Tale (p. 56).—Notwithstanding his hatred of Tyranny, Béranger could not resist the Napoleonic spell. His admiration for the Emperor appears in several of his songs.

The Marquis of Carabas (p. 75).—A stinging satire on

the pretensions of the Bourbon aristocracy after the Restoration.

Poniatowski (p. 89).—Béranger gives the following note on this song:—"Joseph Poniatowski, nephew of the last king of Poland, was born in 1766, and served gloriously in the French armies from 1806 to 1813. After the battle of Leipsic, Napoleon created him a Marshal of the Empire, and gave him the command of a mixed brigade of French and Poles, at the head of which he performed prodigies of valour. On the 18th October, after the bridges of the Elster had been blown up, in order to cover our retreat, Poniatowski, whose brigade formed the rear-guard, though dangerously wounded and pressed by the enemy at all points, positively refused to treat. 'God,' he answered, 'has committed to me the honour of Poland, and to God alone will I resign my trust!' Then plunging into the river, he attempted to make his way to the opposite shore, but overpowered by loss of blood and the fury of the torrent, he was swallowed up and lost. His body was found a few days afterwards on the banks of the Elster."

The Outcast (p. 92).—Béranger's patrician prefix *de* must be borne in mind in reading this song.

A Birthday Letter (p. 95).—The Lilies and the Bees were the emblems respectively of the House of Bourbon and of the Imperial Family.

My Fine (p. 124).—Béranger was sentenced in 1828 to nine months' imprisonment and a fine of ten thousand francs for insulting Chailes X. and the royal family, and offending against public morality. The allusion in line 7 of stanza 3 is to the Holy Water cruse, used at the Coronation Ceremony, which was broken in '93 and mysteriously reappeared on the occasion of Charles X.'s coronation.

The Whipper-snappers (p. 127).—This is given as a specimen of the songs which procured Béranger his conviction. In the original the word "Bourbons" is thinly veiled by that of "Barbons" (greybeards), which has been retained in the translation in order to indicate the objects of his attack. It is impossible to reproduce in English the particular play on the words.

The Refusal (p. 146).—Written in response to an overture from the government of Louis Philippe.

The People's Orpheus (p. 160).—Émile Debraux died in 1831, aged 33. He was the author of "Soldat, t'en souviens-tu!" "Fanfan la Tulipe," and other songs of considerable celebrity, in their day.

My Farewell (p. 177).—Béranger ceased to write for some years before he died. The tailor's shop to which he refers was his grandfather's, where he passed the first nine years of his life.

THE WALTER SCOTT PRESS, NEWCASTLE-ON-TYNE.

Crown 8vo, Price 5s.

"Mr. Toynbee's muse is not afraid to grapple with the more realistic and what used to be considered vulgar topics. If he does not adorn all he touches, he certainly shows that even the most ordinary and nowaday subjects are capable of poetic treatment. The rope-dancer, the agricultural labourer out of employ, the man about town, the thought-reader, the tramp . . . are here invested with true harmony and feeling."—JAMES PAYN, in *Illustrated London News.*

"There is no attempt at fine writing, but there is an admirable attempt, and generally a very successful one, to enter into the lives and thoughts, and express the feelings of the people who are written about."— *The Academy.*

EDEN, REMINGTON & CO.,

HENRIETTA STREET,

COVENT GARDEN.

SELECTED THREE-VOLUME SETS

IN NEW BROCADE BINDING.

6s. per Set, in Shell Case to match.

O. W. HOLMES SERIES—

Autocrat of the Breakfast Table.

The Professor at the Breakfast Table.

The Poet at the Breakfast Table.

LANDOR SERIES—

Landor's Imaginary Conversations.

Pentameron.

Pericles and Aspasia.

THREE ENGLISH ESSAYISTS—

Essays of Elia.

Essays of Leigh Hunt.

Essays of William Hazlitt.

THREE CLASSICAL MORALISTS—

Meditations of Marcus Aurelius.

Teaching of Epictetus.

Morals of Seneca.

WALDEN SERIES—

Thoreau's Walden.

Thoreau's Week.

Thoreau's Essays.

FAMOUS LETTERS

Letters of Burns.

Letters of Byron.

Letters of Shelley.

LOWELL SERIES—

My Study Windows.

The English Poets.

The Biglow Papers.

London : WALTER SCOTT, 24 Warwick Lane, Paternoster Row.

THE CANTERBURY POETS.

EDITED BY WILLIAM SHARP.

With Introductory Notices by various Contributors.

IN SHILLING VOLUMES, CLOTH, SQUARE 8VO.

Cloth, Red Edges	· 1s.	Red Roan, Gilt Edges, 2s. 6d
Cloth, Uncut Edges ·	· 1s.	Pad. Morocco, Gilt Edges - 5s.

ALREADY ISSUED.

Christian Year.
Coleridge.
Longfellow.
Campbell.
Shelley.
Wordsworth.
Blake.
Whittier.
Poe.
Chatterton.
Burns. Poems.
Burns. Songs.
Marlowe.
Keats.
Herbert.
Victor Hugo.
Cowper.
Shakespeare:
  Songs, Poems, and Sonnets.
Emerson.
Sonnets of this Century.
Whitman.
Scott. Marmion, etc.
Scott. Lady of the Lake, etc.
Praed.
Hogg.
Goldsmith.
Mackay's Love Letters.
Spenser.
Children of the Poets.
Ben Jonson.
Byron (2 Vols.).
Days of the Year.
Sonnets of Europe.
Allan Ramsay.
Sydney Dobell.
Pope.
Heine.

Beaumont and Fletcher.
Bowles, Lamb, etc.
Early English Poetry.
Sea Music.
Herrick.
Ballades and Rondeaus.
Irish Minstrelsy.
Milton's Paradise Lost.
Jacobite Ballads.
Australian Ballads.
Moore's Poems.
Border Ballads.
Song-Tide.
Odes of Horace.
Ossian.
Elfin Music.
Southey.
Chaucer.
Poems of Wild Life.
Paradise Regained.
Crabbe.
Dora Greenwell.
Goethe's Faust.
American Sonnets.
Landor's Poems.
Greek Anthology.
Hunt and Hood.
Humorous Poems.
Lytton's Plays.
Great Odes.
Owen Meredith's Poems.
Painter-Poets.
Women-Poets.
Love Lyrics.
American Humor. Verse.
Scottish Minor Poets.
Cavalier Lyrists.
German Ballads.

London: WALTER SCOTT, 24 Warwick Lane, Paternoster Row.

Quarto, cloth elegant, gilt edges, emblematic design on cover, 6s. May also be had in a variety of Fancy Bindings.

THE

MUSIC OF THE POETS:

A MUSICIANS' BIRTHDAY BOOK.

EDITED BY ELEONORE D'ESTERRE KEELING.

THIS is a unique Birthday Book. Against each date are given the names of musicians whose birthday it is, together with a verse-quotation appropriate to the character of their different compositions or performances. A special feature of the book consists in the reproduction in fac-simile of auto-graphs, and autographic music, of living composers. Three sonnets by Mr. Theodore Watts, on the "Fausts" of Berlioz, Schumann, and Gounod, have been written specially for this volume. It is illustrated with designs of various musical instruments, etc.; autographs of Rubenstein, Dvorâk, Grieg, Mackenzie, Villiers Stanford, etc., etc.

"To musical amateurs this will certainly prove the most at-tractive birthday book ever published."—*Manchester Guardian.*

"One of those happy ideas that seems to have been yearning for fulfilment. . . . The book ought to have a place on every music stand."—*Scottish Leader.*

London: WALTER SCOTT, 24 Warwick Lane, Paternoster Row.

THE SCOTT LIBRARY.

Cloth, uncut edges, gilt top.   Price 1/6 per volume.

ALREADY ISSUED.

Romance of King Arthur.

Thoreau's Walden.

Thoreau's Week.

Thoreau's Essays.

Confessions of an English Opium-Eater.

Landor's Conversations.

Plutarch's Lives.

Browne's Religio Medici.

Essays and Letters of P. B. Shelley.

Prose Writings of Swift.

My Study Windows.

Lowell's Essays on the English Poets.

The Biglow Papers.

Great English Painters.

Lord Byron's Letters.

Essays by Leigh Hunt.

Longfellow's Prose.

Great Musical Composers

Marcus Aurelius.

Epictetus.

Seneca's Morals.

Whitman's Specimen Days in America.

Whitman's Democratic Vistas.

White's Natural History.

Captain Singleton.

Essays by Mazzini.

Prose Writings of Heine.

Reynolds' Discourses.

The Lover: Papers of Steele and Addison.

Burns's Letters.

Volsunga Saga.

Sartor Resartus.

Writings of Emerson.

Life of Lord Herbert.

THE SCOTT LIBRARY—continued.

English Prose.

The Pillars of Society.

Fairy and Folk Tales.

Essays of Dr. Johnson.

Essays of Wm. Hazlitt.

Landor's Pentameron, &c.

Poe's Tales and Essays.

Vicar of Wakefield.

Political Orations.

Autocrat of the Breakfast-Table.

Poet at the Breakfast-Table.

Professor at the Breakfast-Table.

Chesterfield's Letters.

Stories from Carleton.

Jane Eyre.

Elizabethan England.

Davis's Writings.

Spence's Anecdotes.

More's Utopia.

Sadi's Gulistan.

English Folk Tales.

Northern Studies.

Famous Reviews.

Aristotle's Ethics.

Landor's Aspasia.

Tacitus.

Essays of Elia.

Balzac.

De Musset's Comedies.

Darwin's Coral-Reefs.

Sheridan's Plays.

Our Village.

Humphrey's Clock, &c.

Tales from Wonderland.

Douglas Jerrold.

Rights of Woman.

Athenian Oracle.

Essays of Sainte-Beuve.

Selections from Plato.

Heine's Travel Sketches.

London: WALTER SCOTT, LIMITED, 24 Warwick Lane.

COMPACT AND PRACTICAL.

In Limp Cloth ; for the Pocket. Price One Shilling.

THE EUROPEAN
CONVERSATION BOOKS.

FRENCH.   **ITALIAN.**

SPANISH.   **GERMAN.**

NORWEGIAN.

CONTENTS.

Hints to Travellers—Everyday Expressions—Arriving at and Leaving a Railway Station — Custom House Enquiries—In a Train—At a Buffet and Restaurant— At an Hotel—Paying an Hotel Bill—Enquiries in a Town—On Board Ship—Embarking and Disembarking —Excursion by Carriage—Enquiries as to Diligences— Enquiries as to Boats—Engaging Apartments—Washing List and Days of Week — Restaurant Vocabulary — Telegrams and Letters, etc., etc.

The contents of these little handbooks are so arranged as to permit direct and immediate reference. All dialogues or enquiries not considered absolutely essential have been purposely excluded, nothing being introduced which might confuse the traveller rather than assist him. A few hints are given in the introduction which will be found valuable to those unaccustomed to foreign travel.

London : WALTER SCOTT. LIMITED, 24 Warwick Lane.

www.ingramcontent.com/pod-product-compliance
Lightning Source LLC
Chambersburg PA
CBHW030605040726
47497CB00008B/2857